The Glass Orchid

Emma Barron

CRIMSON
ROMANCE
F+W Media, Inc.

This edition published by
Crimson Romance
an imprint of F+W Media, Inc.
10151 Carver Road, Suite 200
Blue Ash, Ohio 45242
www.crimsonromance.com

ISBN 13: 978-1-4405-7120-6
eISBN 10: 1-4405-7121-X
eISBN 13: 978-1-4405-7121-3

Cover art © istockphoto.com/DaydreamsGirl; sndr; sx70

Chapter One

London, 1820

Rhys Camden swirled his brandy, watching the amber liquid coat the sides of the glass, slosh over the rim, and soak into the slightly worn carpet of the gambling club.

"I believe you are supposed to drink the brandy, Camden, not wash the floors with it. Though God knows Belford's could use a thorough cleaning."

Camden slowly brought his gaze up from his glass and tried to settle it on his friend, Drew Wittingham, but the man seemed intent on flittering around. Or perhaps it was just that Camden could no longer focus on anything after consuming so much brandy.

"Why *did* we decide to celebrate at Belford's," Wittingham continued, "instead of a more fashionable club? Surely Maven's would have been a more suitable place." Wittingham cast a red-rimmed eye around the club, a look of disdain etching his features as he took in the raucous crowd.

"Well, for one, we aren't members at Maven's."

"Ah, yes. I like to forget that we are not of the highest echelons of society. Pity, really, that even with all of your money you can't just buy yourself a title and be done with it."

"It isn't *my* money," Camden reminded his friend.

"Your money, your father's money." Wittingham dismissed the distinction with a wave of his hand. "It's all the same. Especially since you are now twenty-one and joining the family business."

"And that's the other reason we are at Belford's. Farber decided it was the most s-suitable place for the debauchery sure to occur at my birthday party." Camden's speech slurred and he swayed on his feet as he struggled to focus on his friend. "It's the only place with a reputation worse than his."

"Speaking of the devil, here come our friends now." Wittingham gestured with his tumbler to the two approaching men. "Must have lost at hazard to be back so soon."

Camden squinted. He would have to take Wittingham's word that the approaching forms were their companions; he'd be damned if he could see anything. Then they came close enough that the single blurry shape resolved into Farber and Hollsworth.

"Lost your money so soon?" Wittingham asked.

"Every last shilling," Hollsworth said with a grin.

"Good God, Camden, you look like hell," Farber said loudly as he slapped Camden on the back, causing him to spill the rest of his brandy. "You'll have to clean yourself up by tomorrow morning or your father won't let you in the shipping office. He'd never let such a haggard-looking creature serve as the factotum of his precious business."

"I have plenty of time to clean up before I must report to my father," Camden said.

Hollsworth pulled out his watch. "You have four hours, to be exact." He put the watch back in its pocket and then took in the appearance of his friend. "Not nearly enough time."

"I can't be all that bad."

Farber laughed and slapped Camden on the back again. "Your clothes are stained and crumpled, your eyes are red and blurry, you're looking a bit puffy about that pretty face of yours, and God knows where your cravat's got off to. What an impression you will make on your first day."

Camden frowned. "Perhaps I should make my way home, if I am that bad off. I'll never hear the end of it if I don't show up on time looking presentable."

"Nonsense," Wittingham said. "It is your birthday and your last night of freedom. Beginning tomorrow morning, you are forever cursed to the drudgery of employment. You might as well stay out the entire night and report to your father from here. Daddy will understand."

"Indeed," Farber said. "There is still so much to be done tonight."

"What more is there to do? You've lost all your money," Hollsworth pointed out.

"Yes, but I haven't lost Camden's money yet, so the night is not over."

Wittingham laughed. "Ah yes, how lucky were are that our friend has some of the deepest pockets in London. When we have gambled almost all his purse away tonight, we can spend the rest on whores and liquor."

"Let's not wait on the liquor," Farber said as he peered into his empty tumbler. "I am in dire need of more brandy. As is the birthday boy." Farber grabbed Camden's glass from his loose grasp and turned it upside down. "See?"

"Oh, no, Farber, no more brandy—"

"Right then. First, we get more brandy," Wittingham said, as if Camden hadn't spoken. "Then it's back to the hazard tables." He led the way through the crowd, Farber and Hollsworth close behind.

Camden stumbled along for a few steps but then stopped as a wave of nausea hit him. He had been drinking with his friends since early that evening, and had probably consumed more alcohol in that day than in all the rest of his life. His head pounded and his mouth was horribly dry, as if he had tried to swallow a bundle of cotton rags.

He suddenly wanted nothing more than to be out of Belford's club. It was too crowded and too loud and too chaotic. Too full of groups of drunk and bloated men laughing and yelling as they gambled and fought and chased the club's whores around the floor. He looked around, squinting, trying to find his friends in the blurry mass of black coats, but they had already disappeared into the crowd. It was just as well, he supposed, that he snuck out without telling them. They would never let him leave while the hazard tables were still open and there was still brandy to drink and women to grope. He would have to slip out the side door.

He changed course and pushed his way through the crowd. He pulled out his watch as he lurched along, bumping into furniture and men in his dizziness. He took the watch from its chain and brought it nearer to his eyes, but no matter how hard he squinted, he couldn't make out the time.

"Need some help, love?" a soft feminine voice asked from behind him. Camden turned to find a demimondaine sidling up to him. She was a garish creature, heavily made-up, with a thick coat of powder highlighting the lines of her face and two bright spots of rouge on her cheeks. Her lips were thin and dry, and when she spoke he could see she was missing teeth. "I can give ye the time," she said huskily. "I'll give ye all night."

Camden backed away from her. "Just tell me what that says." He took another step back and put his watch in front of her.

"Almost five," she answered, stepping close to him again.

"Dammit, Hollsworth was wrong. I have only three hours."

"Plenty o' time," the woman breathed. She backed Camden up against the wall, hitched up the skirts of her frayed and crumpled gown, and straddled one of his legs. She rubbed her breasts into his chest, running one of her hands along his torso, stopping coyly near the waistband of his trousers. His watch clattered to the floor.

"I—I must go." Camden pushed past her, not stopping until he reached the side door, and then he burst out onto the street. He stood still for a moment, trying to regain his balance and remember which way to his new townhouse. The residence was a birthday gift from his father, and he had barely moved in. He began walking down the empty street, realized he was going the wrong way, and turned around.

He had only three hours to get home, catch a little sleep, clean up, and report to his father's shipping office at eight. Contrary to what Wittingham thought, his father would most definitely *not* understand if he showed up looking anything less than impeccable and eager to work. Not the father who had once punished him for showing up at dinner with his cravat slightly off center. Not the father who drilled him daily on the importance of appearance and the necessity of increasing the Camdens' social standing to match their great wealth.

Camden quickened his gait, his boots making a sharp clipping noise against the cobblestones, and the sound echoed eerily through the empty streets. It seemed there wasn't another soul out tonight, nothing around him except the faded yellow glow of the gas streetlamps and the cold tendrils of an early morning fog. He heard a loud commotion behind him, a strange thumping punctuated by an otherworldly shriek. He whipped around to see two cats clawing and hissing at each other. He was about to turn back around and continue on his way when another struggle caught his eye. Further down the street, pressed into the shadows, a man clutched at the skirts of a woman. She slapped at him, crying, "You mustn't!" as she backed away. The man grabbed her by the upper arm and pulled her toward him, and Camden could just make out his low growl telling her he could and he would.

Camden was drunk, his vision was blurry, and he had the sensation he was moving through water. He was slow to react to what he saw, and by the time he began to walk toward them, the woman had already broken free. One of her slaps had connected soundly with the man's face and he had released her as he stumbled to the ground. She came running down the street toward Camden, passed him without noticing him, and turned down a dead-end alley. Camden glanced at the man, expecting to see him pursuing her, but he hadn't yet regained his feet. Camden decided he would first find the woman and offer her his assistance before dealing with the man.

He turned into the alley, searching the shadows until he caught movement off in the corner. She was there, standing in a dim halo of gaslight, leaning against the brick wall of a sooty building, one hand against her chest as she struggled to catch her breath.

"Madam," Camden said as he hurried to her.

The woman went still. "You aren't Lord Ashe," she said.

Camden startled at the name. He hadn't realized the man she was struggling with was Lord Ashe. He knew the man—knew *of* him, at least. Ashe was an aggressive and pompous earl who had business dealings with Camden's father. He was a man of dark temper and dark secrets, and Camden wondered how such a beautiful woman had become tangled up with him. "No, I'm Camden—Rhys Camden."

"What is it you want, Mr. Camden? Why have you followed me here?"

Camden stood a few feet from her. He stepped forward and reached for her, but stopped when he saw her draw away. "I'm not going to harm you," Camden said, and though he was trying to be reassuring, his voice sounded thick and strange to his ears. "I've come to rescue you, actually."

He expected a dramatic reaction from the woman; perhaps she would cry in relief or throw herself into his arms in gratitude. He never expected her to laugh. Her slender shoulders shook slightly, causing the fine silk of her gown to tremble, and the loose tendrils of her golden hair to bounce and sway. Camden did reach for her then, his fingertips lightly touching the smooth, cool skin of her arm.

"I'm not in need of rescue," she said.

"But I saw you struggle with Ashe. I saw you slap him and run away. Do not be frightened, madam. I will protect you from him."

A slight smile touched the woman's lips. Camden knew he should be concentrating on assisting her, but he couldn't help but notice how lovely she was. Even in the dim, hazy light of the streetlamp, he could see how the golden curls of her thick hair framed the fine, high cheekbones of her face. His gaze traveled over her plump lips the color of claret, then along the delicate bones of her neck and shoulder, and down to her full breasts. Every part of her telegraphed an ethereal, sensual beauty.

"I assure you," the woman said, bringing Camden's attention back to the present situation, "that I am not in need of any protection."

"But surely—I mean, you cannot—" Camden broke off, confused.

"It is merely a game between Lord Ashe and me, one we often play."

"A game? I do not understand."

"Lord Ashe chases me through the streets, and I struggle and run until I let him catch me."

"What is the point of such a game? To be running through the streets at this hour—"

"The point is pleasure, Mr. Camden." She leaned in closer to him, as if she were going to tell him a secret. "Have you never done anything for pleasure?"

"What can possibly be the pleasure in that?" She was so close to him now that he could feel the heat of her, smell the light scent of lavender on her hair.

The woman laughed again, and she brought a hand up to his arm, her long fingers resting lightly on his coat. There were layers of clothes between his skin and hers, yet a shiver went through him at her touch. "You are so young, Mr. Camden, so innocent," she whispered.

"I'm twenty-one," Camden said, indignant, and he drew himself up to his full height, towering over her by at least a foot. "And I'm not so very innocent."

"Yet your cheeks go red at my touch," she said, and when he started to protest, she stepped closer, until the tips of her silk-covered breasts were touching the wool of his coat. Camden hardened and his face grew hotter. He tried to step back. His erection would be apparent to her if he didn't put some distance between them, but she tightened her grasp on his arm and he found he couldn't move.

She was mesmerizing, this delicate beauty who talked of pleasure and radiated a dangerous sexuality. He was seized with the desire to kiss her, to take her plump lips in his and see if they tasted like wine. He started to lean down to her, and she watched him expectantly, lips slightly parted, until something behind him caught her attention.

"I must go," she said, dropping his arm and stepping past him. "I thank you for your concern, but I am in no need of your help."

"Wait," Camden said, not sure what to say, but knowing he didn't want her to leave.

The woman hesitated for a moment, then turned back to him, stood on her tiptoes, and pressed her lips to his cheek. He reached for her, but she was already moving away from him, her skirts swishing through the fog.

He watched her walk down the alley to the connecting street and then disappear around the corner. He followed her, nearly running down the alley to the corner. He paused, looking up and down the street until he spotted Lord Ashe chasing the woman. Even though she had told him it was just a game, he wanted to go to her and save her from her pursuer. He started to move toward her but then sank back into shadows when Lord Ashe caught her about the waist and turned her around. They were far enough away that he couldn't make out the expressions on their faces, but he could see now from the way they moved with each other that she truly didn't need his protection. She shrieked and slapped at Lord Ashe when he grabbed her, but she leaned in closer to him as she did so. Lord Ashe took her by the arms, holding her firmly, but Camden could see that there was no real roughness in his touch.

Camden knew he should leave them. They were standing down the street in the opposite direction he needed to go, and he could slip away without drawing their notice. But he found himself rooted to the spot, intrigued by this strange game played in the empty streets before dawn by a beautiful woman and a powerful man.

Lord Ashe backed the woman against a building, and said something to her in a low, husky tone. Camden saw one of Lord Ashe's large hands run up the bodice of the woman's gown, saw him run a finger along the neckline and over the curve of her breast. Camden drew in his breath, shocked that the couple would engage in such behaviors in the middle of the street, even if there were no one about. Then Camden saw Lord Ashe's bring his mouth to the woman's neck, kissing her almost aggressively.

Camden felt a strange mixture of horror and curiosity as he watched Lord Ashe thrust his hips toward the woman, lifting her off the ground. He was not completely lacking in experience with women, but none of his admittedly few encounters had prepared him for the sight of a man and woman engaging in illicit behavior on the street, in plain view of anyone who happened to come along. As an overly reserved and proper young man, he'd never thought to conduct himself in such manner; before tonight, it hadn't occurred to him that *anyone* would think to do it.

He stiffened again, shamefully aroused at the sight of the woman, at the sound of her sighs and moans as she clutched at her lover. Camden ached to touch the woman as Lord Ashe touched her, to sink himself into her, to taste her, to hear her cries against his ear—even as he was horrified at the very thought of fondling a woman in the street. The couple's movements became more frenzied, until Camden wondered if he would take her right there, but then Lord Ashe backed away from the woman, setting her gently on the ground. He removed his coat and put it around her, then leaned down to her, and Camden thought Lord Ashe said,

"Let's finish this at your townhouse," as he put an arm around her waist and propelled her down the street.

Camden stood in the shadows of the street, his erection throbbing, his head pounding. He shouldn't have watched them, shouldn't have been aroused at the sight of their passion, shouldn't stand here thinking about her until he burned with unmet need. But the image of Lord Ashe and the nameless woman was still seared in his mind, and it wouldn't let him go. The couple had disappeared, yet still he stood, staring down the empty street until he became convinced it had all been just a drunken dream.

Chapter Two

Adele Beaumont brushed a stray curl from her eyes, smoothed her gown, and slipped a gloved hand around the arm of her companion, John Blakely. Blakely smiled down at her and then pulled her closer to him so they would not collide with another couple passing them on the sidewalk.

"Jane Montel always has the best supper parties, don't you think, Del?" Blakely asked as they walked along.

"Her parties are always exciting, and this one was no exception," Del said. "I think it must be because she is an actress. It gives her the ability to make every gathering a production, complete with drama and intrigue."

"I think you've got it. Always some grand conflict unfolding, some dark secret revealed, or some such thing. I've come to rely on it. But I never would have guessed Mare Winschel and William Hawkins were having an affair. Quite a shock when Mrs. Hawkins walked in on them in the study, wouldn't you say?"

"How could you not know they were involved in an affair? They've been carefully ignoring each other in public for months, yet they always seem to disappear at the same time at every party. It was so obvious."

Blakely laughed. "So their lack of interaction with each other was a sure sign of their relationship?"

"To anyone with eyes it was," Del replied, rolling her eyes in mock exasperation. "You men miss the most blatant clues."

"And you women are forever reading epics into the smallest looks or gestures. It is like some secret code or something—one that no man has the hope of ever deciphering."

Del smiled mischievously. "Oh, so now you would blame your complete inability to comprehend society on the entire female sex? How typical, to deny that any of the confusion is due to your own shortcomings."

Blakely stopped walking. "There is nothing short about me," he said as he swung Del around to face him. He drew her to him, his green eyes glinting wickedly as he pressed against her. "You should know that by now."

"Do behave yourself, Mr. Blakely, we are on a public street. I would positively faint from mortification if anyone were to see us in this unseemly embrace."

Blakely laughed again, not fooled in the slightest by Del's seemingly earnest warning. "You've never given a damn what people thought, and you never will. And the day I see you faint is the day the world stops spinning on its axis. But here, I will unhand you. We are approaching your townhouse anyway, and I would much rather grope you in there than out here."

"Take heart, Blakely. If the world were to stop spinning on its axis, it would finally be free to start revolving around you instead, as you've long believed it should." Blakely began to reply to her comments, but Del cut him off. "As to my townhouse, let me find my key, and we will see what transpires."

Del opened her reticule and began to search for the brass key that unlocked her front door. She had a habit of putting as many things in the reticule as it could hold, and the small key seemed to always be hiding among the various objects. Blakely moved behind her as she searched, slipping an arm around her waist and pulling her closer to him. He nuzzled her, pressing light kisses along her neck.

Del looked up from her reticule. "Blakely, please, you are not making it any easier to find my key. If you would just—" She broke off, her gaze locking with that of a young man across the street. He was staring at her, unmoving except for his dark blond hair that stirred in the breeze. He looked at her with the same sort of confused expression on his face that she knew was showing on hers—and Del knew they were both trying to place each other. She recognized that angular face, that tall, lanky build of a young man who had not yet completely filled out, but she couldn't remember where she had seen him.

"If I would just what, my dear?" Blakely said as he ran a fingertip along the low neckline of her gown.

"If you would just—" Del didn't notice she had trailed off; she wasn't really paying attention to what she or Blakely were saying. She had finally remembered that the young man across the street was the Mr. Camden who had tried to rescue her from Lord Ashe several weeks ago. She remembered how earnest he had been when he came to her, how innocence and the smell of brandy had clung to him like palpable entities.

Del saw recognition dawn in Camden's eyes, saw a blush creep up his neck, and she found herself wanting to laugh, to go to him, and to scurry into her townhouse all at the same time. She saw his eyes flick to where Blakely's hand rested on her gown, and then up to Blakely's face, and when Camden's blush intensified she knew he had just realized that it was not Lord Ashe who was embracing her. A strange sensation rippled through her, and it took her a moment to realize it was the unfamiliar feeling of embarrassment. But why should she care if Camden had seen her with both Ashe and Blakely? He was nothing to her, this tall stranger with the last traces of childhood still clinging to his lean frame and soft eyes. She would simply turn away from him and break the piercing gaze that seemed to root her to the ground, as soon as —

"Del? What's wrong?" Blakely's voice finally caught her attention.

"What? Oh, nothing—just searching for my key—" Del looked down at her reticule, saw the glint of fading sunlight off brass, and triumphantly held up her key as she turned around to face Blakely. She tried to focus only on him, but the hair at the nape of her neck rose, and she knew Camden still stared at her. "Let's go inside."

Blakely searched her face for a moment and then looked beyond her to where Camden was surely still standing across the street. Del took Blakely's arm, drawing his gaze back to her, and she led him up the stone stairs to her townhouse. "You may wish to stand on the sidewalk all evening, but I am going inside," she said.

Del fumbled as she hurriedly tried to fit her key in the lock. She felt strangely exposed there on the steps, like her deepest secrets had been unearthed. With a sigh, she told herself to stop being ridiculous. She finally managed to unlock the door, and quickly ushered Blakely inside, eager to shut the door on Camden and his unsettling stare.

"What has gotten into you?" Blakely asked. "You seem so distracted. Is it something to do with the man—"

"Nothing has gotten into me," Del said as she peeled off her gloves. She threw them and her reticule onto the mahogany side table. "I am going to go change out of my gown. Why don't you go into the study and pour us some brandy? I need something to wash the taste of Jane's gin from my mouth."

Del started up the stairs before Blakely could respond. By the time she reached her bedroom, she had already removed the pins from her hair, and was shaking the blonde curls loose until they fell down around her shoulders. She struggled out of her gown, corset, and chemise, and then slipped into a red silk robe. She turned to go back downstairs, carefully avoiding the full-length mirror that stood near the door of her bedroom. She didn't want to catch a glimpse of herself, didn't want to see how the passage of time had stamped fine lines around eyes dimmed by too much experience. She wasn't exactly in her dotage yet—she was only twenty-eight—but the weight of a difficult and complicated life often made her feel much older than her actual years.

Del slowly descended the stairs, the marble risers cool against her bare feet. Although she tried to confine her thoughts to the fact that Blakely and brandy were waiting in the study, she found they kept drifting to the look on Camden's face when he recognized her. But why should he be stuck in her mind? Why should she be thinking of this young man—this mere child—when an old friend sat waiting just down the hall? Del shook her head as if to physically wipe Camden's image from her mind, and went to the study.

Blakely was indeed waiting for her, sitting on the settee, holding a brandy tumbler in one hand while the other idly plucked at the burgundy upholstery. He shifted when he heard her come in, and then leaned casually against one of the settee's arms. Del walked over to the sideboard, took the glass of brandy Blakely had poured for her, and went to sit in the wingback chair opposite the settee. She took a long sip of the brandy, peering at Blakely over the rim of the tumbler.

This was the man that should be occupying her thoughts. Blakely was everything Camden was not: he was broad shouldered, with steely muscles that flexed and strained against the fine wool of his coat. He had none of Camden's gawkiness, none of that golden innocence. Blakely moved with cool assuredness, radiating power and grace and a wealth of experience. Where Camden's mien was a reflection of his guilelessness, Blakely's dark hair, gleaming green eyes, and the ever-present hint of stubble that lined his hard jaw telegraphed a mysterious sense of danger that Del had always found exciting. Yet it was Camden, this young man she didn't even know, that she was suddenly picturing underneath her, with his large hands running over her naked body.

She grew warm at the images in her mind, her nipples hardening until they chafed against the silk of her robe.

"Rather introspective tonight, aren't we, dear?" Blakely asked.

The picture of Camden dissolved and vanished at the sound of Blakely's voice. "My mind does seem to be wandering," Del said.

"Come, sit next to me," Blakely said as his gaze traveled to where Del's robe gaped open, revealing the curve of one breast and her nipple still hard from imagination. "I'll banish all wayward thoughts and replace them with dark and wicked ones."

Del sat silent for a moment, watching Blakely's gaze rove over her body. Then she stood, and murmured "not tonight" as she walked over to the sideboard to pour herself more brandy. She heard him approaching her, and then he pressed against her, pinning her against the sideboard. One of his large hands snaked around to her belly, untying the sash of her robe and pulling it open, exposing her bare skin to the cool evening air. Without thinking, she spread her legs and arched her back, and Blakely thrust against her until she could feel him harden.

"My God, I want you," Blakely said against her ear as his hands cupped her breasts, lifting and squeezing until they ached from pleasure.

Del felt him pull away from her, and she realized he was fumbling to open his breeches. Her body reacted instinctively with anticipation. She began to pull her robe up to her hips, and was about to murmur his name when she froze, letting the silk fall back around her ankles.

It hadn't been Blakely's name about to tumble from her lips at all, but Camden's. Dear God, why could she not get him out of her head?

"I can't do this tonight, Blakely," Del said, her voice raspy, as she quickly retied her robe. She grabbed her brandy from the sideboard and went back to the chair to sit down.

"Bloody hell," Blakely spat, panting in frustration, his brows furrowed and his hands fisted at his sides. "I want you."

"That's most apparent," Del said, looking pointedly to where his erect cock still strained against his breeches. "But you know our arrangement, what you agreed to before you ever decided to consort with me. You know that I am not obligated to have sex with you if I choose not to."

"Not that—well, yes that," Blakely said as he adjusted his breeches. "But that's not what I meant."

Confused, Del looked at him, her gaze following him as he walked stiffly back to the settee and sat down on its edge. "What did you mean, then?"

Blakely leaned forward, and Del knew he wanted to come to her, to touch her or sit next to her. But he didn't, and Del could see how hard he struggled to keep himself in check. "I want you to myself," he said, his gaze steady. "I want you to give up all the others."

Del blinked, taken aback. "Blakely," she said, and her tone made it sound like a warning. "You know that is the last thing I want."

"I could offer you security," he said quickly. "I could you give you all the financial support you need, whatever you want."

"But I notice matrimony is not on the table."

Blakely paled, swallowed hard. "If that's what it takes…" he said, his voice strangled.

"Oh my." Del laughed. "The consummate bachelor Blakely is actually proposing marriage? Don't scowl at me, Blakely, engagements should be a joyous occasion."

"Dammit, Del—" Blakely started to rise from the settee, but Del raised a hand to stop him.

"I can't—I won't put myself at the mercy of any one person." Del's tone had turned serious. "I've worked too hard, struggled too much for my independence and freedom to just throw it away. To put myself in the one situation I've spent my life trying to avoid."

"Blast you and your damned independence. Is it really worth so much that you will cling to it at the exclusion of all else?"

Del bristled. "What else is there that matters?"

"How about security? How about companionship? Or love?"

"You know I love you, we've been dear friends for almost a decade now."

Blakely gave a rueful laugh. "We're friends, yes, but I doubt you even know what love is. You are so careful to keep people at a distance, with all of your stupid 'arrangements.' And you will *never* let anyone in, will you? You hide here in this damned townhouse, all alone, no servants or anyone about, only taking visitors on your own terms, and pushing anyone away who tries to get too close."

"I am not alone," Del said, carefully schooling her features to appear light and flippant. "I always have Mrs. Tiddles to keep me company and keep me out of trouble."

Blakely's face darkened. "There you go, making stupid jests to avoid any uncomfortable conversation." He squinted at her for a moment, looking as though he wanted to shout at her and only the barest thread of self-restraint stopped him. "Your imaginary great-aunt does not actually count as a companion," he said finally, his voice soft and carefully controlled. "Though how you've managed to fool everyone with that silly ruse and convince them you are merely a respectable woman living with her aunt is beyond me."

"I manage to fool everyone because people *want* to be fooled. They see what they want to see and believe what they want to believe." She sounded almost angry, or perhaps it was just a note of practical resignation that had turned her voice hard. "Denial must be the most powerful force on earth; it makes all unpleasant truths disappear. It makes the poor and sick invisible, it makes the nobility useful, and it makes whores into respectable women." Del gulped her brandy, coughing and wiping the sticky liquid from her lips. She shifted in her chair, only now noticing the silk robe had fallen open, exposing her long legs up to the thigh. "In any event, society does not concern itself so much with a twenty-eight-year-old spinster who keeps to herself, not when there are so many more important rich and titled children to keep track of."

They regarded each other in silence for a moment, both frustrated, both wary.

"You will never allow it to happen, will you?" Blakely said, his voice low and quiet.

Del arched a brow. "Allow what?" she asked.

"You will never allow anyone to love you. You will never let your defenses down." Blakely got up with a jerk, and walked over to the side table to pour more brandy. He grabbed the decanter with a clenched hand, brandy sloshing over the rim of the tumbler as he poured it.

"You are so untouchable," he said as he returned to stand in front of Del's chair. "Like an orchid under glass. Beautiful, exotic—and forever out of reach. But someday, someone will come along who will shatter the glass, who will ignore the jagged edges and reach inside and grab you. And you will be powerless to stop it." His gaze slid from hers, and he peered into the tumbler, as if searching for some elusive answer marinating at the bottom. "God knows I'm not brave enough to attempt it." He gave a sort of helpless laugh, and then anger seized his features. He threw his tumbler against the far wall and stalked out of the study while the shards of glass still rained down to the floor.

Chapter Three

"Why I let you drag me to these low-class soirees of yours, Farber, I will never know." Wittingham smoothed his wool coat as he walked, picking at an invisible speck of lint and straightening his already impeccable cravat.

"Because deep down in that snobby little heart of yours, you know you love them," Farber said with a laugh as he poked Wittingham, causing his friend to frown and smooth his coat yet again. "You enjoyed the other party you attended at Jane's. And you are as eager as I to force Camden here to have a bit of fun." He gave Camden a playful shove.

"I am the epitome of fun," Camden said sardonically.

"Not since you started your employment," Hollsworth piped up from behind the group. "You haven't gone out a single night since you started working for your father. Not very nice of you, really, to leave Farber without funds to lose at the hazard table."

Farber turned to scowl at Hollsworth. "I have been doing just fine in the funds department, thank you," he said, not quite mustering up any plausible indignation.

"Yes, you have been doing quite well since you took up with that silly chit of an actress," Wittingham said. "What's her name? Millie? Mary?"

"Mare," Farber said.

Hollsworth laughed. "Yes, since you've been riding—"

"No, don't do it," Wittingham admonished. "I cannot abide any poorly crafted allusions to Farber and his activities with his equine-monikered mistress." Wittingham turned to look at his friend, and when it looked like he was about to say something else, Wittingham raised a hand to cut him off. "I mean it, Hollsworth, enough with your bad puns and horrible jests." Once satisfied that

Hollsworth wasn't about to spout out another one of his famously cringe-inducing jokes, Wittingham turned back to Farber. "Really Farber, I should be quite used to your antics by now, but to allow some woman to support you…that seems too base for even you."

"I may allow her to give me a shilling here and there, but I give her plenty in return," Farber said as he cupped the front of his breeches. "Almost more than she can handle," he added with a smug a laugh. Behind him, Hollsworth snorted gleefully at the innuendo.

"You do realize that makes you a common prostitute, don't you?" Wittingham said, the edges of his lips curling up in a poorly concealed smirk.

Farber's expression was suddenly devoid of smugness. "I—I'm not—"

"You're a whore!" Hollsworth yelled, laughing louder. He gave Farber a shove, causing him to stumble before he shoved Hollsworth back.

Leaving the two men to scuffle harmlessly behind them, Wittingham turned to Camden. "Worthless cads," Wittingham muttered, but Camden heard the note of brotherly affection in his tone that belied his harsh words and haughty demeanor.

"They're just young, and too fun-loving for their own good," Camden said with a glance back at their friends. Farber now had Hollsworth's head under his arm, clamped tightly to his side, and Farber mussed his hair while Hollsworth yelled, "Let go!" and, "Ouch, dammit!"

"I suppose we were like that once," Wittingham sighed, slowing his pace so Farber and Hollsworth wouldn't fall too far behind. "But then things happened to make us abandon our carefree ways—like you becoming employed and me being older than ten."

Camden grinned. "You can't fool me, Wittingham. You aren't nearly as priggish as you pretend to be."

"No, I'm far worse. I suspect it is my advanced age—"

"You're only twenty-five!"

"Yes, but sometimes those six years that separate me from them—" Wittingham made a vague gesture in the direction of Farber and Hollsworth, "—seem more like decades."

"Really, Wittingham, you'll have yourself in the grave before you're thirty."

"And perhaps it will be not a moment too soon. Ahh, I believe this is the townhouse." Wittingham said before Camden could respond. He stopped walking and turned to Farber, who was still scuffling with Hollsworth. "Stop that, man, and tell me if we've found the place."

Farber released Hollsworth from a headlock and squinted up at the townhouse. "This is it," he said. "This is Jane's house."

Farber leapt up the stairs and rapped on the door. It opened a moment later, noise and cigar smoke seeming to tumble from the house and pour out onto the street.

"Jane!" Farber said in greeting to the woman who stood in the doorway. "You've missed me, haven't you? Fear not, I have finally come, and look, I've brought Wittingham, Camden, and Hollsworth."

"And now the party can finally begin," Jane said flatly. There was the sound of breaking glass, and the voices behind her swelled into raucous laughter, as if the people inside were in on the joke.

"Perhaps the party has already begun," Farber said, unfazed by Jane's sarcasm, "but at least now it can get *good*."

Jane turned her gaze from Farber and looked over his friends. Camden felt strangely exposed by her inspection. She was an unsettling creature—one who seemed to reside in the twilight of unclassification. She was attractive, yet none of her features taken singly would be pleasing in themselves. Her eyes were too large, her nose too long, her jaw too severe—yet it all added up to an arresting whole. She was poised, almost regal, but as an actress,

Camden knew she couldn't have come from well-bred stock. Her voice was slightly too high pitched to be strictly pleasant, yet she spoke with such seductive authority that Camden thought there would be few who would hesitate to obey her every command.

"If you are the missing ingredient to a perfect party," Jane said, drawing her gaze back to Farber, "then I suppose I should not deprive anyone of your presence for a second longer." She stepped inside the doorway, and gestured for the men to come inside, taking coats and hats and canes as they passed.

Camden followed his friends through the hallway in to the main parlor, his eyes nearly tearing up from the thick smoke. There were clusters of people throughout the house, talking, drinking and laughing. Nearly all the men—and not a few of the women—were smoking something, a pipe, a cigar, what appeared to be pieces of rolled up paper filled with tobacco. There were card tables throughout the room where animated foursomes played whist or vingt-et-un. A few couples danced a most scandalous waltz to the slightly discordant sounds of a rather inebriated-looking quartet folded into a dark corner of the parlor. Other couples were pressed into the shadows, pressed into each other. Camden caught glimpses of exposed flesh and roving hands. In all, Camden thought the party seemed pungent, loud, crowded, a bit shocking—and horribly fun. The kind of fun Camden hadn't experienced in the month he had been in his father's employ.

"Amazing, isn't it?" Farber asked, and Camden saw he was grinning stupidly and rubbing his hands together, as if the party were some great feast he was about to tuck into. "And to think Wittingham, that you complained about coming. What you would have missed." Farber turned his idiotic grin on his stoic friend, who only raised an eyebrow in return. "Ah, look, there's Mare. Come, Hollsworth, and I'll introduce you to Mare's pretty little friend."

Camden watched as his two friends disappeared into the crowd in pursuit of more titillating attractions than either he or Wittingham could provide.

"Worthless cads," Wittingham pronounced for the second time that evening.

Camden laughed. "You will have to come up with some new insults. You are starting to become repetitive. Wouldn't want anyone to think your biting wit was going soft."

"It's just that it's so apt," Wittingham said, and although the light was low, Camden could have sworn the man was smiling. "But enough of them. I am going to enquire as to what lengths a man must go to procure spirits of some kind. I certainly need the fortification. You coming?"

"Excellent idea," Camden said, but as he turned to follow his friend, something caught his eye that rooted him to the spot, and he barely noticed that Wittingham had moved on without him.

Standing in the shadows across the room was the blonde beauty he had stumbled across the night of his birthday, and saw again a few weeks later. She looked tonight as tempting as she ever had—more so, perhaps. She was in a dress of red silk, a shock of color in the dim room. She seemed finer, more delicate, more beautiful—more *alive*—than anyone else in the room. Her hair was gathered and pinned up, exposing the long, delicate lines of her neck. A neck that Camden wanted to press his lips against before moving down to the hollow of her collarbone, and then down yet more to the soft mounds of flesh straining against a plunging neckline. Camden's pulse pounded in his ears, and his cock stiffened painfully against his trousers.

"Stunning, isn't she?" asked a voice beside him.

Camden jerked slightly, startled at the sudden intrusion into his thoughts, and saw that Jane had come to stand beside him. "I—she—er—who—"

"Del," Jane said with a nod toward the blonde sylph. "The most mysterious woman in London."

Though he tried to avoid it, his attention turned back to the woman—Del—though he knew he must look the fool, gaping after her stupidly. "And who is she, exactly?" he asked Jane.

"I'm not entirely sure," Jane replied. She caught the perplexed look on Camden's face. "Oh, I've known her many years, dined with her, sought amusement with her, but I can't say that I really know her."

Camden never took his gaze from Del, but he knew his expression must have reflected his reaction to Jane's words, how little he cared for such cryptic speeches.

"I see you are not satisfied with such an explanation. I shall simply have to introduce you to her then, so you can see for yourself." Before Camden could stop her, Jane caught Del's attention and gestured for her to join them. Camden watched as the smile of recognition that lit Del's face as she saw Jane froze as she realized who was standing next to her. Caught, she began to move toward them, for she couldn't ignore the summons of her hostess without giving unpardonable offense.

Camden panicked. "No, really, I don't want to trouble…that is, I must find my friend Wittingham…he was off to find a drink, and I…" Camden began to turn, hoping to execute a hasty exit, but Jane's firm hand on his arm stopped him.

"Nonsense," she said. "What sort of hostess would I be if neglected to make the proper introductions between my guests? Ah, Del," she said, giving her friend a quick embrace as she joined them. "Adele Beaumont, I'd like you to meet Rhys Camden."

Del hesitated for a moment, the slightest of smiles touching her lips. "Mr. Camden and I have met before, although it was an all too brief encounter." Del turned her full gaze upon him, and Camden noticed for the first time the startling color of her eyes. They were hazel flecked with green—emeralds bathed in whisky—and Camden wanted to drown in them.

"Have you?" Jane said, eying Camden suspiciously. "I was under the impression you did not know each other."

"We—it was as Miss Beaumont said. A brief encounter on the street—" Camden blanched as he heard the coarseness of his explanation. "I did not even catch her name at the time."

"Quite so?" Jane asked archly, her eyebrows raised.

Camden reddened under Jane's inquiring look. He thought back to that night, what he had witnessed with Del, and realized Jane, knowing under what circumstances her friend normally met with men, imagined *he* had been the one with Del. He reddened more as he began to imagine the same thing, summoning decadent visuals of himself locked in a rocking embrace with the beauty before him. He abruptly cut off his thoughts when he realized both women were looking at him quizzically.

"It was nothing, Jane," Del said, as if she sensed Camden needed rescue. "A chance encounter several weeks ago. Camden was under the mistaken impression I needed assistance finding my way home."

"Oh?" Jane infused that single syllable with such skepticism that Camden knew she didn't believe the encounter had been that simple at all.

Camden was about to defend himself when Del spoke. "You will have to forgive me, Jane," she said, "but I find I am unusually fatigued tonight. I'm afraid I must beg my leave. Thank you, though, for a lovely evening. Your parties, as always, are full of surprises." Before either of them could protest, Del gave a quick kiss on the cheek to Jane, a quick nod to Camden, and then she turned and left the room.

Camden knew he should let her go, that chasing after her would be the height of madness, that it would serve only to fuel suspicions of others. He should forget her, this strange woman who seemed to appear suddenly like an apparition, the mere sight of her stirring up lust, curiosity, and something else, something he couldn't identify or name.

Hadn't he always been told that ungoverned passion was a sign of weakness? It was undisciplined, uncouth, unworthy of a man of his current station—and certainly of the station his father hoped the family would one day occupy. A man's entire person, his thoughts, his actions, his emotions, should be kept firmly in check. He should never take rash action, never give careless expression to his feelings. He had been told that often enough. Indeed, he could hear his father's voice now, in his head, telling him those very things.

He couldn't say what it was then, what unseen force pulled him or what unheard of stroke of rebellion pushed him to abruptly turn from Jane and nearly run out of the room after Del.

• • •

Del's chest constricted as she struggled to get air. She was furiously working to locate her pelisse, reticule, and gloves from the pile of outerwear in the front hall, thinking that if she could just leave the townhouse and step out onto the street, she would be able to breathe freely again. She heard footsteps behind her and she knew without turning who was coming after her.

"Mr. Camden," she said without turning around, pleased that her voice sounded calm and even. "Have you forgotten something? Come to say good-bye, perhaps?"

She waited for his response, and when none came, she frowned. Perhaps it hadn't been Camden who had followed her into the foyer. But no, turning around, she saw it was indeed the young Mr. Camden who stood just inside the hall, his face slightly flushed, his hands fisted at his sides.

Neither of them spoke for several ticks of the longcase clock standing in the corner. That audible passage of time mixed with the pounding of her pulse in her ears to create the only sound in the room. Del felt strange, uncomfortable. How disconcerting it was that every time she laid eyes on this stranger it should affect her so. She had always thought herself so calm, so poised and in control. And yet here she was, practically panting for breath and fighting an urge to turn and run from the house.

"Miss Beaumont," Camden said finally, "I—I wanted to speak with you." He shifted his weight, clenched and unclenched his fists. "I wanted to tell you—"

Del took a step toward Camden. Whatever he meant to say to her caused him obvious discomfort, and it piqued her curiosity.

"I just wanted to say I can assist you," Camden said in a rush. "I can help you with your—er—situation."

"And what 'situation' would that be?"

Camden reddened. "With the men—what I saw that night— I—I have money. Money and a few connections. If you need anything—" He broke off, looked away from her.

Del wasn't sure how to react to his statements. It certainly wasn't the first time a man had offered to "save" her. Yet this was different. He didn't know her, didn't have any arrangement with her, and, unlike every man who had come before him, he didn't seem to be making his offer solely in exchange for exclusive rights to her.

"Mr. Camden," Del said slowly, "you are very kind. But I meant what I said to you that night we first met: I am not in need of any sort of rescue. I've chosen my life and I'm happy with it as it is. I am not looking for you or any other man to save me from it."

"But no woman chooses that!" Camden looked at her again, his confusion showing clearly on his face.

Del smiled. "I assure you, I have. And why should that be so difficult for you to believe? Why are you so concerned?"

Camden looked startled that she should even pose such a question. "It—it is a sin! An affront to God!"

"God?" Anger rose in her breast. "God abandoned me long ago when He took my parents from me as a child, left me with no one but cruel or indifferent relatives who passed me around—" Del broke off, surprised and angry that she let her emotions overcome her, that she would so recklessly blurt out her secrets. She took a deep breath, deliberately calmed herself. "I am not so concerned with God's judgment. It seems He has already done His will."

"And society? Have you written that off as well?"

Del laughed outright at this. "Again, Mr. Camden, I am hardly able to rouse myself to care about currying favor with a society that has so completely left me to fend for myself." She said this simply, without bitterness or rancor. "Well, I am doing just that: taking care of myself through the only means available. And society seems to care little, so long as I am discreet."

"But there are rules—right and wrong—societal dictates to be followed lest chaos ensue—"

"Oh? But even you, Mr. Camden, do not always follow said dictates. Come now, don't look so shocked at the suggestion. That night we first met, when you came to my aid, you know you had no right to interfere in a domestic spat between a man and a woman, whether it's his wife or mistress."

"But that was different! I was drunk, and you were struggling trying to get away." Camden stepped toward her. They were only a few inches away from each other now. "I know Ashe and what type of man he is; I couldn't have very well left you."

"But that is exactly what society says you should have done. So you see, Mr. Camden, we all do what we think we should, what we are compelled to do, what circumstances demand we *must* do." Del took a step back, his nearness as unsettling as his questions. He looked at her so earnestly, as if he genuinely cared what she had to say for herself, as if he really wanted to help. It confused and distressed her.

He looked at her so intently, his soft brown eyes locked on hers. She wondered what he must think of her now that he knew for certain what she was, what she did. Then she wondered why should she care, when no one's opinion had mattered to her before. Why now? Why this man? Del slid her gaze from his and focused on the longcase clock ticking in the corner. She had hoped breaking eye contact would also break the strange, breathless hold he seemed to have on her, but she could still sense his gaze upon her, feel his body next to hers. Suddenly, Del wanted—needed—to get away. Away from the party and its noise and boisterousness. Away from the leering gazes of drunken men. And most importantly, away from the disconcertingly concerned and generous Mr. Camden.

"Forgive me, I—I was just leaving and I—" Del turned her gaze back to Camden, but she kept it hovering in the vicinity of his chin. She couldn't bear to see disbelief and worry and disapproval mingling in his eyes, and she cursed herself for her cowardice. Many years ago, when she decided to take charge of her own fate, she had promised herself she was done with cowering, with evading and disassembling in an attempt to apologize for who she was and the fact that her existence placed such a burden on her long-suffering relatives. She had vowed to look away from no man, and yet here she was, standing in a foyer listening to the gonging of a clock and the slightly hitched breathing of a young stranger, and she could not meet his eye.

Del moved toward the door, her gloves still off and her pelisse draped over her arm. Camden's hand was suddenly on her elbow, causing Del to freeze as she sucked in her breath. She had been touched by dozens of men, in manners far more familiar and salacious, and yet *this* touch, by *this* man, was far too intimate.

"Mr. Camden, please—" Del forced herself to look him in the eye. "I really must be leaving."

Camden looked at her, his brows furrowed, and Del knew he wanted to say more to her, that he struggled with whether to give voice to any affirmation or reproach that might be swirling in his head, or whether to remain silent and let her leave. Del decided to make the choice for him. She wrested her arm from his hand and was out the door before Camden had a chance to react.

Chapter Four

"Blakely came to see me, you know," Jane said as she linked her arm with Del's.

Del stumbled just then, though surely it was on a bit of loose gravel on the path and not because of Jane's words. Jane's arm stiffened as she helped to steady Del, but she continued walking without comment.

"Oh?" Del hoped her voice sounded casual, that it belied none of the intense curiosity she actually felt.

Jane gave her a sideways glance and Del knew her attempt at nonchalance had failed.

"It seems he is quite worried about you." Jane's eyes scanned the path. She seemed almost bored with the present conversation, and appeared instead to be intently studying the other pedestrians enjoying the sunny afternoon in Hyde Park. Del knew, however, that Jane was thoroughly enjoying her playful torment.

"Worried about me?" Del said with a soft laugh. "Whyever for?"

"He said it has been weeks since you—how shall I put it? Been *in flagrante delicto*, and days since you have entertained him at all. He pleaded with me to make you see reason."

"Pleaded? Blakely has never pleaded—"

"Oh no you don't," Jane said with a good-natured laugh. "You will not focus on my diction and ignore the substance of what I said. I will not let you maneuver out of an explanation that easily."

"There is nothing to explain. I have merely been busy, and I haven't had the time to see Blakely."

"Busy with what?" Jane asked, clearly skeptical.

"Well, I—Mrs. Tiddles and I—"

Jane gave a most unladylike snort before she abruptly stopped walking and turned Del to face her. "Ah, so there *is* something going on with you! You only bring up the mythical great-aunt when you are trying to conceal something."

"Nonsense. You are being ridiculous."

"Del," Jane said, her tone completely serious for the first time that afternoon. "We have been dear friends for years. Tell me what has you so distracted lately, what has you shutting out your companions."

"Really, Jane, you are being dramatic. We are not on the stage." Del started walking again, threading her arm back through Jane's and pulling her along. "I am simply taking a little time to myself, that is all." Del almost smiled at how convincing she sounded. Her composure—her armor—was firmly back in place.

"Blakely's worried you've agreed to be exclusive with someone. Put him in quite a fettle, that notion, considering you rejected *his* offer."

Del scoffed. "You know I would never make such an arrangement."

"So it wouldn't be a certain handsome young man you met weeks ago causing this rift, then, would it?"

Del stiffened slightly before she could catch herself, and she hoped Jane hadn't noticed. "Young man?" she asked, a paragon of innocence. Blast Jane and her perceptiveness.

"The blond gentleman you saw at my party last week. The one you had apparently had—'dealings' with before. The one who made that impeccable façade of yours crack oh-so-slightly, and caused you to bolt rather unceremoniously from my townhouse into the night. That one."

"I'm sure I don't know what you mean. I was simply tired that evening and left a little early."

"You may be able to keep men at a distance with your deft dissembling, my dear, but not me. Never me. Who *is* he?"

Del hesitated, wondering just how much she should divulge to Jane. And, really, what was there to tell? Rhys Camden was nothing more than a man—a young, innocent, idealistic man—who'd spotted her on the street and tried to intervene when he thought she needed saving. Tried to help again when he thought she needed to escape her life. It was no different from a dozen other young men who had tried to "save" her, who had offered Del their protection in exchange for exclusivity. Except Camden hadn't demanded her services as payment for his heroism. He didn't seem to want anything in return for helping her.

And now Del couldn't get him out of her head.

The images came to her unbidden, his sweet earnestness when he came to her aid that night with Lord Ashe. How he had looked at her, a mixture of interest and desire and innocence and awe showing so plainly on his face. How he had touched her, so gently, with hesitation and something akin to reverence. How his wish to help her had battled with his aversion to what she did, what she was, when he came to her at Jane's party and offered her a way out.

She saw him everywhere. She would catch a glimpse of a tall blond man on the street, and her heart would jump until she looked closer and realized it wasn't Camden. Someone would call her name on the street, and when she felt a surge of disappointment upon seeing who it was, she knew she had been hoping it had been him. It was his face she saw in her mind, late at night, when her body ached for another person's touch, and when she finally fell asleep, frustrated and alone, she dreamt of him.

It terrified Del, this preoccupation, this wanting that she couldn't seem to control. Men had always been a means to an end for her, a way for her to escape the indentured servitude of a penniless orphan dependent on the goodwill of merciless or indifferent relatives. She had always been able to keep men at a distance, to use them as they used her. Even Blakely, whom she was genuinely fond of, had been thus far unable to penetrate her defenses, though he seemed intent on trying. So what was it about Camden that made him affect her in such a manner? What made him take over her thoughts and dreams and desires? She was so consumed with Camden since seeing him outside her townhouse she had been unable to be with anyone else. She knew she risked everything by putting a hold on her arrangements. The men would soon tire of waiting for her and would turn their attentions to someone else. Someone younger and more pliable, more easily dealt with. But still she could not bring herself to see anyone.

Del was struggling with what to reveal to Jane and how to put her confusion into words, when a strangled gasp escaped her lips as she suddenly spotted the object of discussion. Rhys Camden was just ahead on the path, mounted atop a large chestnut stallion, as if her thoughts about him had conjured him into being right before her. He was dressed as properly as ever, with a conservatively cut tailcoat and impossibly snug nankeen breeches, but his cravat was loosened slightly and his hair was a bit disheveled. He was wearing an expression Del had never seen on him before: carefree contentment. His gloved hands held the reins loosely and his bearing was relaxed. The breeze tousled his hair, causing the longish strands to curl around his high collar. Del saw the hard lines of his muscles flex against his breeches as his thighs gripped the horse. He looked almost happy, and it was such a stark contrast to his usual stiff and formal demeanor that Del almost gasped again.

Del realized she had stopped walking and now stood in the middle of the path gaping stupidly at Camden, Jane still hanging on her arm. If she did not move, Camden would ride right past them, seeing them, and Del could think of nothing she wanted less than to converse with him right now, especially with Jane studying her every expression.

"Oh, Jane, I just remembered I wanted to show you the new roses in Kensington Gardens," Del said as she turned around abruptly, dragging Jane with her. "They're just back this way."

Jane glanced behind them, and with a sly smile she withdrew her arm from Del's and stopped walking. "Oh! I seem to have a bit of gravel stuck in the sole of my walking boot. I'll just be a moment to fish it out." She bent down to her shoe, her skirts billowing out behind her, and inspected her—suspiciously unobstructed-looking—sole.

Del tugged at Jane's arm, desperate to get away from Camden. She thought they still might be able to escape his notice if they hurried, but then she heard the jangle of the horse's bit right behind her and knew it was too late.

"Mr. Camden," Jane said warmly as she rose to her feet. "What a happy surprise to see you."

Camden reined in his horse, stopping so close that Del could feel the beast's breath on her still-turned back.

"Ma'am," Camden said, and Del heard the bewilderment in his voice. He seemed not to remember Jane and must be wondering why she addressed him by name.

"I was just asking Del when we might see you again," Jane said.

Del had no choice but to turn around and acknowledge him now. She curtsied as he nodded to her. She noticed with perverse satisfaction that he was blushing fiercely, which seemed only right since her own heart pounded and her breathing was uneven. Good that he was as discomfited as she.

"Miss Beaumont," Camden said, his voice sounding slightly strained. "I hadn't expected to see you again."

If it weren't the height of rudeness, Del would have informed him she hoped that had remained the case. She wanted this man out of her thoughts and out of her life so she could carry on as usual, without emotional embroilment, unwanted attachments, or impossible desires. But she couldn't very well forget about him if he kept popping up everywhere she went.

"Mr. Camden," Del said in what she hoped was a friendly yet disinterested voice, "this is indeed an unexpected meeting."

Camden looked as though he wanted to say more to her, but he glanced at Jane and remained silent.

Jane clearly understood his reluctance to speak to Del in front of her. "Oh goodness!" she exclaimed. "It quite slipped my mind that I was to meet with my dressmaker for a fitting this afternoon. You wouldn't mind seeing Del home, would you, Mr. Camden? I really must go."

Jane was already hurrying down the path away from them, giving Camden hardly any choice but to agree. He dismounted the stallion and gathered the reins in his right hand, motioning to Del with the other to show him the way. His familiar rigid formality was back in place; that glimpse of a more joyous Camden so brief and so completely replaced, Del wondered if she had imagined it.

Del forced herself to walk calmly beside Camden, and she fought the urge to run down the path away from him, as if fleeing some great horror. She told herself to stop being ridiculous. He was a man and nothing more, certainly not anything to engender such wild impulses. She couldn't seem to stop feeling unsettled and vulnerable whenever he was around, and it was that—that ungoverned *feeling* of anything—Del suspected she was actually trying to run from.

"I am glad to have crossed paths today," Camden said, finally breaking the awkward silence. "I have been thinking of the last time we met, at the party." Camden cleared his throat, and Del could tell how uncomfortable he was. "I must apologize."

Del's head snapped up. She looked at Camden closely for the first time since they started walking. "Apologize? For what?"

"For what I said to you, for presuming you needed or wanted my help." Camden glanced at her quickly before returning his gaze to the path before them. "It wasn't my intention to cause you discomfort."

"Mr. Camden, I—" Del realized with some astonishment that she had absolutely no idea what to say. She tried to recall the last time a man had apologized to her or shown concern for her feelings, much less regret for upsetting them, but she drew a blank. "I assure you there is no need to apologize. The entire incident is hardly worth mentioning."

"Yes, well, still—I apologize for my familiarity."

"Thank you," Del murmured, though she wasn't sure Camden heard her, because the sudden gleeful shriek of a child running across the path caused his stallion to snort and stomp sideways, drawing Camden's attention.

"Whoa, gentle, Sebby." Camden laid a calming hand on the horse's muzzle.

"He seems rather spirited," Del said.

"Yes, he is," Camden said as he stroked the horse. "He's barely civilized. In fact, most days it is a question of whether he deigns to allow me to pretend I am the master and ride him at all."

Del smiled at the note of playful affection in his voice. "You seem almost more at ease with the horse, belligerence and all, than you do with people." She had only meant to tease him, but he nodded earnestly.

"Quite so," Camden said with a laugh. "His motivations are far easier to understand: eat, sleep, run, mate, perhaps fight the other stallions to demonstrate his strength and secure his position."

"Ah, but that doesn't sound so very different from most men of my acquaintance."

Camden laughed again. "Perhaps not, but at least the horse doesn't lay pretense to loftier ideals."

"True," Del said, "men often claim they are motivated by honor and conscience and a desire to achieve a greater good, when really they all seem to be nothing more than rutting beasts fighting for a bit of power."

"You don't seem to carry a very high opinion of the male sex."

"It seems no lower an opinion than you hold for them."

"Perhaps not."

"Then tell me, Mr. Camden, what has so tainted your esteem of your fellow man?"

Camden shrugged, and though the gesture was casual enough, Del detected a hint of tension in the action. "People will look for any advantage over you, and go in for the kill the moment they can. A smart man will strike first and give them no opportunity to best you."

Del looked up at him, her eyebrow raised. "Strong words, but you don't sound completely convinced of them."

Camden shrugged again and looked straight ahead. "I have been told those words often enough, I may as well believe them."

Del wanted to press him further, but his tone told her he wasn't eager to remain on the subject. She was curious, though, as to who'd drilled such a harsh sentiment into him and what part it all played in forming his stiff reserve, if any. She would get no answers today though, she knew. They walked along companionably, and Del began to feel more at ease. They exited Hyde Park and turned down the street that would bring them to Del's townhouse, though they were still some blocks away. Camden walked in the street, leading Sebby, pressed against the curb to allow mounted riders and carriages to pass him while Del stayed on the sidewalk.

"Your house is just this way, if I recall," Camden said.

Del nodded in affirmation. She realized Camden had not asked for further direction since leaving the park. It surprised her that one chance encounter in front of her townhouse weeks ago had left enough of an impression on him that he could lead her home now with no hesitation.

"I'm afraid you have me at a disadvantage, Mr. Camden."

"How so?"

"You know so much about me—where I live, my associates… what I do." Del could practically hear Camden's nervous gulp at the mention of her profession. "And yet I know nothing about you." It wasn't until Del said it that she realized how uncomfortable this inequity made her. She was used to thoroughly vetting any and every man she came in contact with, all the while carefully guarding her own privacy.

"What is it you wish to know?" Camden asked.

"Well, let's see. You told me when we first met that you are twenty-one. I also know that you like horses more than people and you enjoy offering to rescue ladies in distress. Don't blush, Mr. Camden, I'm only teasing you."

"I'm not blushing," Camden said as he turned a darker shade of red.

Del decided not to embarrass him further. "What do you do, Mr. Camden? For a profession."

"I serve as factotum for my father's shipping company."

"And what does that entail?"

"Anything and everything my father needs. I am learning all the details of the business since my father hopes I will take over the company when he is gone."

"He hopes? It doesn't sound as if you are overly eager to fulfill his wish."

"I will do my duty," Camden said, and Del noticed how clenched his jaw was after he spoke and how tightly he gripped Sebby's reins.

Del guessed from his reaction that Camden had a tense and complicated relationship with his father, and she wanted to know more. She could hardly pry into such an intimate arena, however, no matter how brightly her curiosity burned. "Navigating family ties can be difficult." Del kept her tone sincere yet light, hoping to simultaneously convey her understanding and deflect some of the tension. "I suspect my great-aunt Mrs. Tiddles would be similarly demanding, if she weren't made up."

"Indeed. Wait—what?" Camden stopped walking and looked at her, clearly perplexed.

"Mrs. Tiddles, my great-aunt and benefactor with whom I live. I made her up."

"Why would you invent a fictitious relative?" Camden asked as he began walking again.

"Well, I can't very well force society to acknowledge reality, now can I? The grand dames of London would rather live as peasants—can you imagine the horror?—than have to admit there is an orphaned whore living and supporting herself among them. Mrs. Tiddles allows everyone the comfortable fiction that I am a respectable woman living off the proceeds of a generous relative. Oh, Mr. Camden, you are blushing again. Have I positively scandalized you?"

"No—well, yes," Camden said, laughing. "But I could do with a bit of scandal. I'm just a bit taken off guard. You are terribly candid, aren't you?"

"I don't see the point in prevarications. I am sorry if I have shocked you."

"I should be shocked, and yet I find you—refreshing. Most of society, myself included, spend their lives gossiping and scheming, saying only what others want to hear, what will achieve their aims and desires. And here you are, utterly forthright and without pretention. I find you very intriguing."

Del's cheeks grew warm, and it seemed it was her turn to blush from embarrassment. She saw with relief they were approaching her townhouse and she would soon be delivered from Camden's presence. The conversation was veering into entirely too uncomfortable territory, and she was grateful for escape. She removed her house key from her reticule and started up her front steps.

"Thank you, Mr. Camden, for escorting me home. You have again proven yourself a gentleman."

"Miss Beaumont, I—" Camden shifted, clearly uncomfortable.

"Yes, Mr. Camden?" Del asked, wondering what, exactly, he meant to say. It wouldn't be a proper Camden encounter unless he said something surprising to her.

"I was hoping I—that is—I would like to see you again," he said. "Not for—I mean, not as a—" Camden cleared his throat as he struggled to come up with the properly delicate phrasing.

Every impulse Del had screamed at her to mutter her apologies and then flee into the house, forever shutting the door on Camden and the complications he represented. She didn't need this, didn't need the uncertainty and confusion and awkwardness that swelled within her whenever he was near. Instead of running, though, she found herself saying, "This Friday. Jane is playing Miss Maria Dorrillon in her theater's production of *Wives as They Were and Maids as They Are*. You may come round at seven to collect me."

Camden smiled as he bowed to her. "Until Friday then, Miss Beaumont." He mounted his horse and trotted off, melting into the heavy traffic of the street and disappearing from view.

• • •

Del flicked her wrists, the delicately carved ivory blades of her fan clicking together as she desperately tried to create some small relief from the theater's stifling, muggy heat. The lobby was a sea of muslin and silk, satin and kerseymere, the women and men inhabiting the materials scarcely distinguishable in the crowd. Camden's hand was strong and warm on her back, anchoring her to him so they wouldn't be separated as everyone jostled to get into the gallery before the play began.

She saw a few familiar faces around her. She smiled warmly and tipped her fan to her friends and acquaintances, and she politely pretended not to see or know the several former "suitors" who were there with their wives or new mistresses. It was this adeptness at both gracious acknowledgment and serene detachment—either so easily given depending on what the situation required—that had helped secure her position as a sought-after companion of the wealthy and powerful men of London. One such man caught her eye, and her face froze as she quickly brought her fan up higher to obscure her expression before her celebrated composure left her entirely.

Lord Ashe stood not ten feet from her, his tall, broad frame allowing him—along with Camden and a few other men—to rise above the heads of the generally shorter crowd. Del stiffened with surprise and discomfort. She hadn't seen Ashe in weeks, not since that night when Camden had tried to rescue her from him, and she was unprepared to see him now. Ashe had tried to contact her since then, sending increasingly demanding missives to her house practically ordering her to accompany him to some event or another. He knew, of course, that Del did not respond to demands or orders, and any hint of such only strengthened her resolve to ignore them and the person issuing such insults to her autonomy.

She tried to ignore him now, but he was a handsome, imposing figure whose bearing and demeanor drew the attention of even the most reluctant observers. He stood near one of the lobby's large, ornately turned columns, wearing a coat of deep blue crushed velvet, a chateau bras tucked smartly under his arm. He took a few steps forward as he walked along with the crowd, and his companion, previously obscured by the column, came into view, causing an inexplicable sense of ire to swell within Del. She recognized the woman clinging to Ashe's arm as Sarah Wilson, the courtesan most recently taking London by storm. She was young, barely eighteen, and though attractive it was supposedly her wit and vivacious charm rather than any unmatched beauty that drew men in. She had been on the scene for barely a year, but she had already secured her reputation as alluring, magnetic, and feisty, with acumen for the business of seduction far exceeding that of any of the other much more seasoned courtesans currently working the salons and opera houses of London.

Del felt another twinge of emotion, and though she would never admit it to anyone, she knew it to be jealousy tinged with fear. It wasn't that *she* wanted to be the one murmuring in Ashe's ear—she had been studiously avoiding that lately—it was that she didn't want *Ashe* to want someone else on his arm. She hated seeing the evidence of her replaceability, hated being reminded of the tenuousness of her life. She had worked hard to ensure a measure of independence for herself, supporting herself the only way she could, but seeing Ashe now demonstrated how easily her fortunes could change. All it would take was the distraction of the newest ingénue, and like a once shiny object stripped of its luster, Del would be discarded in favor of the new toy and soon forgotten. And what would become of her then?

Her disquieting thoughts were interrupted when Camden leaned down to her, his lips brushing against her cheek. "You are stunning this evening," he said against her ear.

Del shivered, she couldn't stop herself. His breath was warm on her neck, his husky voice like a caress, and it sent every one of her nerve endings buzzing. "Do behave yourself, Mr. Camden," she said with a playful swat of her fan against his arm.

"What? I merely paid you an innocent compliment," he said teasingly.

"Yes, but the *way* you said it was anything but innocent." She gave him a devilish smile.

Camden pulled her against him. "I confess my motivations are perhaps not completely pure. Something about you makes me want to be a bit wicked."

Del's pulse quickened. She was used to flirting with men—it was her livelihood, after all—but she normally did it in a rote, automatic manner, with no attached feeling or even overly great interest. Flirting with Camden, however, was completely different.

This was far from the mechanical exchanges she normally engaged in, exchanges carefully designed to pique the interest and desire of the client. She found herself responding to him quite against her will. When he touched her, her skin heated; when she felt his breath against her ear, she shivered. And when the young, guileless, and normally reserved and ever-proper Camden looked at her with a glint of hunger in his eyes and told her she made him wicked, her heart pounded. It made her quite forget herself—her past, her future, her present surroundings.

She had almost completely forgotten Ashe and his new companion until she caught a glimpse of him from the corner of her eye. He was staring at her now, irritation tinged with anger showing plainly in his dark expression. He must have seen the exchange between her and Camden, must have seen the way he stood so close to her, his arm snaked protectively around her waist. Ashe would have also seen how Camden made her react, how she blushed at his words and leaned in closer to him. Maybe Ashe could sense the crackling electricity flying between them, maybe when Del's heart jumped and the attraction flared, it produced visible lightning bolts for everyone to see. It certainly felt as though it could.

Del knew Ashe well enough to know why seeing her with Camden made him angry. She had been refusing to see Ashe, avoiding him without explanation, and now here she was, at the theater with another man. Ashe was accustomed to having his demands met, his desires catered to, and it was an unpardonable affront to his position and power for Del to ignore Lord Ashe in favor of the young, untitled, and comparatively unimportant Rhys Camden.

Ashe pulled away from Miss Wilson and took a step forward looking as if he was determined to fight his way through the crowd and confront Del and Camden. Ashe was aggressive and impetuous; he would think nothing of creating a scene or even engaging in a physical altercation in the middle of the theater. Del moved toward the gallery doors in earnest, no longer content to drift along with the crush of people heading toward their seats. She was eager to put more distance between them and Ashe, though the crowd made forward progress difficult.

"In a hurry, are we?" Camden asked.

"I don't want to miss the beginning," Del said. Camden clearly hadn't noticed Ashe glowering at them from across the room, and Del wanted to keep it that way. "Jane would never forgive me."

Nodding, Camden stepped forward, grasped Del's hand, and led them into the gallery. He didn't jostle or push anyone, he merely drew himself up to his full height and claimed space around them, seeming to effortlessly clear a path to their seats. Del glanced behind her and was relieved that Ashe was no longer visible. The crowd had swallowed them, and there would be no confrontation this evening.

Camden found their row and led Del to their places, carefully stepping around the patrons already in their seats. Suddenly, he stopped short, and his hand clenched around hers. His abruptness caused Del to bump into his broad back, and she was about to ask him what was wrong when he nodded stiffly to a gray-haired gentleman seated before them.

"Mr. Hutchence," Camden said in curt acknowledgment.

"Mr. Camden," Hutchence said, returning the nod. His eyes flicked over to Del, and they widened in surprise. Del was passingly familiar with the man; she had seen him at various salons and similar outings. She was quite sure he recognized her and knew her for what she was, and she thought she detected an air of censure at Camden's choice of theater companion.

They were saved from further conversation when the gas lamps dimmed, and they moved quickly in order to be seated before the play began.

"Are you very well acquainted with Mr. Hutchence?" Del asked as they took their seats, hoping to discover the source of the tension-filled greeting between the two men.

"He's a business associate of my father's," Camden said.

Del wanted to ask him more, but the footlights brightened, the curtain opened, and all conversation stopped as Jane entered the stage. Del tried to concentrate on the play, but her thoughts kept intruding. She was unbalanced, like a ship listing in the open sea after a squall, rudderless and without purpose. Being with Camden, she felt emotions and desires she thought she had long since abandoned. She wanted to know him, and not just in the perfunctory, utilitarian way she normally gathered information on men to facilitate and maximize her business dealing with them. Normally, she confined herself to such details as a man's favorite food and colors, his daily habits, whether he preferred brandy or port, how he took his tea, and other equally mundane tidbits.

With Camden, she wanted to know so much more, from the mundane to the weighty. What was his childhood like? Was he a quiet, amendable boy or was he naughty? What caused his contentious relationship with his father? Was it always thus, or did the relationship recently deteriorate? Were his dealings with his mother equally fraught? Camden didn't seem eager to join his father's shipping business; what dreams did he hold for himself instead? What were his political leanings, and did he think the Cato Street conspirators were purposely entrapped? Why did he reign himself in so tightly when Del had caught glimpses of him in unguarded moments and knew a fiery spirit burned inside him? She wanted to know it all. She wanted to know why he looked at her with such an agonizing mix of tenderness, desire, and bewilderment. Why he had offered her so much and asked nothing in return. Most importantly, she wanted to know why he stirred such ungoverned emotions and engendered such baffling reactions in her.

Camden was dangerous, she realized. He made her want to let her guard down, to let him into her heart and her life, even knowing how vulnerable that made her. She caught herself having dreams of normal life—of marriage and houses in the country and perhaps a child or two—even though tonight had demonstrated how out of reach that life was. She could never escape her past, never fully divest herself of the Ashes and the Blakelys of her world who thought they had a claim to her, who thought she owed them her companionship until they themselves called a halt to it. And Camden, he could never escape the expectations of his position in life. She had seen the frosty exchange between him and Mr. Hutchence, saw the opprobrium in Hutchence's glance and the way Camden stiffened in reaction to it, and she knew that there was no possible future for them.

However strong the forces of attraction were that drew them together, the bonds of society that held them in place would always be stronger.

Chapter Five

Camden sighed heavily as he ran an ink-stained hand through his hair and fought the urge to tear it out in chunks. The night grew late and the other employees had long since left the shipping offices, but he was still sitting at his lamp-lit desk going through the books. It was quiet, dark, and utterly still. Camden hadn't seen or heard another individual in hours, and though he knew it was ridiculous, he felt as though every other person had ceased to exist and he would be here forever, alone in the world, sitting at his desk going numb from the tedium of the business accounts.

He wondered what Wittingham, Farber, and Hollsworth were doing while he sat there alone and bored. He imagined they were already in their cups, gambling away their money and chasing girls of easy virtue. He could almost hear Farber's drunken laugh as he ribbed Hollsworth, and he could perfectly imagine Wittingham's practiced disdain of their antics. Though he often grew tired of Farber's and Hollsworth's excesses, right now he wanted nothing more than to be with them, far away from ledgers, bills of lading, and the specter of his father.

Though he was not now physically present in the office, the elder Mr. Camden's judgment and reproach seemed to inhabit the building like an angry ghost. Camden never felt fully free of him, and he knew his father wanted to make sure that was the case. Reminders of him were everywhere, from his tersely worded notes of instruction littering Camden's office to his father's portrait hanging on his walls. Even rendered in colored oils, his father appeared to be glaring at Camden, clearly communicating his ire. And like the beady-eyed paintings in a gothic novel, his father's eyes seemed to follow him everywhere, noting—and inevitably disapproving of—his every movement.

"You are still here. Good."

Camden looked toward the office doorway and thought grimly that the tired phrase "speak of the devil" had perhaps never been so apt. His father stood dressed entirely in black silk, as if in mourning—the death of all cheerfulness and enjoyment, most likely. Although it was still fashionable to allow one's hair to fall in a few untamed curls or waves, Mr. Camden had wrestled his locks into meek submission and his hair stuck tightly to his scalp, as if the slightest hint of unruliness signaled an unstoppable march into pure decadence. Everything about the man was stiff, somber, and controlled.

Camden straightened in his chair and self-consciously smoothed his own disheveled coif. "Yes, I'm still here. Just finishing the last of the day's accounting."

"You have finished the receipts and filed the bills?

"Yes," Camden said, putting down his pen. His father sounded more gruff than usual, if that were possible, and Camden wondered what sort of dressing-down he was about to receive.

"You have not been shirking any of your duties to the company, have you?"

"No, of course not."

"You remember where your loyalties lie, do you not? To the company, to me, to the family."

Camden nodded and said nothing, though he wanted to demand what this interrogation was all about. He knew better than to open his mouth, however. One simply did not demand answers of George Camden. One waited until George Camden deigned to enlighten you.

"You were at the theater a few nights ago, were you not?" His father walked into the room and stopped a few steps from Camden's desk. He was not an overly tall man—in fact, he was several inches shorter than his son—but George Camden was so domineering, his stance so stiff and erect, his gaze so intense, that he seemed to inhabit far more space than what his physical self actually occupied.

"Yes, I was at the theater," Camden said. He began to suspect what had his father questioning him so aggressively.

"Tell me, who accompanied you?"

"A—friend," Camden said carefully.

"A friend?" His father said, and Camden heard the note of derision in the question, as he knew he was meant to.

George took a few more steps forward and placed his hands on the desk. They were thick hands, roughened by work and struggle and ambition. Every callus was a map of a past marked by grinding poverty and stark deprivation. Every cut and bruise was a beacon of the grueling labor he undertook to elevate his fortunes. Every ink stain and smudge of grease was a promise of the even loftier position he hoped to one day attain. A position George expected his son to also strive for.

Camden forced himself to bring his gaze from his father's hands and meet his eyes. He would not let himself squirm like a naughty schoolboy awaiting his punishment. He would not stammer and blink as he tried to explain himself to a father who demanded repentance at the slightest perceived indiscretion but would never give understanding or absolution.

George pushed back from the desk and walked over to the far wall, inspecting the various portraits and framed documents hanging there, as if he were merely engaged in a friendly chat. "I went shooting the other day with William Hutchence," he said, and Camden was not fooled by the air of casualness in the statement. "He is also a theater-goer, apparently." He gave a slight emphasis to "theater-goer," as if the activity were something vaguely distasteful.

Camden said nothing.

"He saw you there," George continued, his back to his son. "With a woman." He turned to face Camden, his hands clasped behind him. "You were seen with the same woman in the park at least twice. Once before the play and once just yesterday."

"Are you having me followed?" Camden blurted before he could stop himself. He hadn't meant to say more than necessary—no use providing any extra length of rope with which his father could hang him—but his father's detailed knowledge of his whereabouts was a disconcerting surprise.

"Followed?" George scoffed. "No. It is not necessary to have you followed. I have told you again and again you must guard yourself at all times. There are always people watching, waiting for you to acquit yourself in a manner that belies your origins, that proves we are not worthy of moving beyond our humble station." George began to pace the small office. Camden could see redness creeping up his father's neck and knew he was becoming increasingly agitated.

"I don't think—"

George slammed his hands down on Camden's desk, cutting him off. "Dammit, Rhys!" George said, the oath another indicator of his loss of composure. "After all I have done, after all the work and the sacrifice to achieve what we have! For you to just throw it away by appearing out in public—multiple times!—with that—that—*whore*!"

"She's not—"

"Do not try to deny it! I have been apprised of who and what she is. It is one thing to discreetly visit one in the darkness of night, if you must. But to be seen in general society with such a creature, to defile the family name this manner—I will not allow it."

Camden's instincts warred within him. He wanted to leap from his chair and come to Del's defense. He wanted to yell that she wasn't a whore or "creature" and he wasn't defiling anything when he was with her. He wanted to command his father to leave him alone, to finally accept that his son was an adult and fully capable of living life without constant interference. But those impulses were tempered by years of being trained—by sharp glances, harsh words, or even a beating if necessary—to obey his father. George Camden demanded compliance in everything, great and small, and nothing was greater than his desire to achieve a level of social respectability to match his newly made wealth. Camden knew his father would abide nothing that threatened to quash his upward progress.

"Are you even listening to me?" George snapped, leaning over the desk. "You are not to do or say or even *think* anything that could endanger our reputation or your eligibility for a suitable marriage."

"But I don't want—"

"This is not about what you want! We have more money than most of the blue-blood lords in this country—hell, half of them are indebted to me for more money than their crumbling estates can ever hope to repay—and yet still they balk at aligning their families with ours."

Camden hated it when the subject of marriage came up, and it came up with alarming frequency ever since he'd turned of age. George was convinced the final step to social grace was his son marrying into one of the families—and there were many—who possessed the good name, breeding, title, and respect George desperately craved but who, perhaps through generations of peevish idleness and estate mismanagement, currently lacked the wealth the Camdens could provide. And so Camden was expected to enter into a marriage that amounted to little more than a business transaction. He would exchange money for respect and finally gain the entrance into the highest levels of society that had thus far been unattainable by George.

Camden knew what he must do, and yet the prospect of such a marriage, of such a cold and loveless life, filled him with dread. He had seen it first hand, had witnessed how decades of empty duty and barely veiled contempt of each spouse for the other had weakened and finally ravaged his mother, ultimately sending her to her grave a few years back.

He didn't want that.

He wanted more, though he had never given himself leave to entertain what *more* would even look like.

"You are never to see that woman, nor any other person such as her, again."

Camden opened his mouth to give the expected words of acquiescence, but then stopped himself. He was flooded with images of Del. Of her running through the darkened streets, breathless and mysterious and beautiful. Of her walking in the park with him, teasing him with jests and shocking him with honesty until he felt the mortifying blush of embarrassment flush his cheeks. Del at the theater, her lovely face softly lit by the glow from the footlights as she raptly watched the performance. How her entire countenance lit up with mirth as she laughed along with the crowd. How afterward she had surprised him with astute commentary on the social and gender implications of the play. He thought of all this, and he knew he couldn't make any promises to his father.

He wouldn't be able to stay away from her.

Camden brought his gaze to meet his father's, saw how red and mottled his face had become. He knew there was a rage building in his father that would soon boil over, and still he couldn't force himself to say the words that would stem the angry tide.

"What is wrong you, boy?" George's voice cracked slightly and Camden knew he was barely hanging on to his control. "What possible charms could this whore possess that make you even think of defying me and destroying everything I have worked so hard to build?"

Though phrased as a question, Camden knew his father's words were meant to be an accusation, not an inquiry. The man had no real interest in what made Del so intriguing, but Camden found himself wanting to try to explain it to him anyway. What could he say, though? How could he make his father understand what made Del so different? She was extremely intelligent, wholly independent, and so completely without pretense that it quite literally took his breath away at times. How could he phrase it so it would make sense to his father? Camden wasn't sure George even understood the concepts of independence or disregard for social intrigue and machinations.

"She is—different from any person I have ever met," Camden said.

George's eyes bulged, and Camden knew he was both surprised and enraged that Camden had actually tried to explain himself. "Different?" George shouted. "*Different*? You would squander our fortunes and reputation on the childish notion that this whore is somehow *different*? Let me tell you something, boy, there is nothing special about her. Nothing. She is nothing more than a common whore that can be bought of any street of London."

"She's not a common whore," Camden said as he began to rise from his seat. "She's—"

"*Enough!*" George yelled as he slammed his hands down on Camden's desk. Camden instinctively sat back down, hardly aware of what he was doing. "I am through speaking with you on this matter. It is over. No more. You are not to see her again. Ever."

Camden looked down at the papers scattered across his desk and said nothing.

"Do you understand? Never again. Hear me?"

"Yes," Camden and though he was defiant, he was still not ready to give voice to his complete thought. *Yes, I hear you, but I make no such promises.*

George glared at him for several seconds, and Camden felt the heat and weight of it, as if his anger were a corporeal being ready to physically strike him. And then it was gone as George stalked out of the office, his father seemingly satisfied that he had procured a promise of obedience from his son. He had no reason to believe otherwise. Camden had thus far always done as he was told, behaved as he was expected. And parts of Camden wanted to do that now, wanted to stave off any further conflict by doing what his father ordered. He should cease all contact with Del and redouble his efforts at the shipping company. Then his father would be happy—or at least not overtly furious; Camden doubted his father was ever actually happy—and Camden could continue living his rote life in relative peace.

He just—couldn't. There was something in him, some small spark that became a little more inflamed every time he thought of Del, which prevented him from meekly submitting to his father's demands. Yes, he could avoid any contact with her and buy himself a reprieve from his father's fury, but he was beginning to think the price he paid—had been paying his entire life—was becoming more than he could bear.

He stared down at his desk until the numbers in the ledgers blurred, and he knew he would get no more work done tonight. He rose abruptly, toppling his chair over and scattering papers, but he was too frustrated to care about setting his office back to rights. He grabbed his coat and left the shipping offices. He needed air, needed to move, needed time to think. He would walk the streets until he was calmer, and then he would return to his office to finish the accounting.

Even as he stormed down the streets following a now-familiar route, he still pretended to himself there was some question as to where he would end up that night.

• • •

A cool evening breeze blew in from the open window, causing the delicate silk curtains to billow and ripple on the current. Del drew her robe closer around her as she closed the book on her lap with frustration. She had been trying all evening to read the over-wrought gothic romance but she was having difficulty focusing. She found herself reading the same paragraph over and over again, and when she was finally able to read through an entire chapter, she was plagued with a distraction of a different kind. Every time she encountered a description of the aggressive raven-haired hero sweeping the heroine into his arms, he somehow changed into a soft-spoken blond man in her mind. Somehow, it was Camden she envisioned storming the haunted mansion to rescue the quivering maiden.

Del tried to banish such ridiculous images from her mind, but her mind refused to cooperate. It conjured memories of Camden, of his eyes peering into hers, his voice soft against her ear, his hand strong and firm on her back. It created visions of him. Camden riding on his horse as she had seen him yesterday afternoon in Hyde Park, except in her head he was wearing no cravat or waistcoat, and his linen shirt was open to the waist, exposing his muscled chest.

"Ugh, stop it," Del told herself.

She rose from the settee and went to the sideboard to pour a tumbler of brandy. She took a gulp, reveling in the warmth that burned a trail down her throat. She wiped the sticky liquid from her lips with the back of her hand and went to sit back down, the half-full tumbler still clutched in her fingers.

She simply had to stop thinking about Camden, had to stop romanticizing who he was and what they could be together. She had thought in the beginning it was simply curiosity. He had intrigued her with his young innocence tinged with a hard, still-burgeoning masculinity. It had caught her off-guard how forthright he was with her, how he treated her as a person with desire and needs, and not just a vessel to fulfill his lust. She had agreed to accompany him to the theater because she thought that if she spent time with him the alluring sense of newness and mystery would wear off and she could go back to the way she was—independent, in control of her own destiny, free.

Instead, she had been left wanting more. She wanted more time in his presence, more quick-witted conversation, more of the stolen glances and small touches neither of them could curtail. The encounters with Ashe and Hutchence and shown her how futile it was for her to pursue even a friendship with Camden, and yet she couldn't bring herself to stay away from him. He had come round her townhouse the day before and suggested they take a stroll through the park, and she hadn't been able to stop herself from agreeing. She had tried, it had been on the tip of her tongue to tell Camden they could no longer see each other, in any capacity, but the words had died in her throat. It was as if someone else, a person who wasn't struggling to defend herself against the vagaries of fate and society, had overtaken her and it was that person who told Camden in a far too eager voice that she would love to spend the afternoon with him. Again, she told herself the lie that she would soon tire of him, that her interest would be sated and she could walk away from him. And once again the falsehood was revealed at the end of the afternoon when, as Camden had walked her home and she had dallied at her door, she was loathe to leave him.

Del was pulled back to the present by a sudden gust of cold wind and the sound of rain pelting her townhouse. She hurried to the window and shut it before the rain could soak her carpets. She was about to pour herself more brandy when she was stopped, decanter held mid-air, by an insistent knocking on her front door.

Blakely, she thought as she entered the foyer. She knew he would show up at her door eventually and demand to know why she had been avoiding him. She wondered what she should tell him, because it certainly couldn't be the truth. She wasn't even ready to fully admit it to herself—that she hadn't been able to be with anyone because her mind had become too crowded by thoughts and memories of Camden. That it felt somehow wrong to be with a man that wasn't him. She would have to eventually, she knew. She couldn't be with Camden and she couldn't support herself staying shut up in her townhouse, alone.

She put her hand on the knob, ready to disarm Blakely with a dazzling, if not altogether sincere, smile and some carefully spoken platitudes. Her smile froze and any witty remark flew from her head as soon as she opened the door, however. It wasn't Blakely standing on her step.

It was Camden.

His great coat was pulled tight around him to ward off the wind and rain, and his hat was pulled down low on his brow, nearly concealing his blond hair, but Del knew instantly who it was. She had replayed her memories of him often enough to know his stance, the way he stood with his feet apart and his head tilted slightly to the left. She knew him by his long, strong fingers holding his coat close around his neck, by the squareness of his shoulders, his height. She knew she could identify him by the smallest part.

He looked up at her, his dark brown eyes on hers. "Del," he said simply, softly, and she could tell something had upset him. She had seen him ungoverned once before, when he was riding his horse in Hyde Park. It had been unrestrained happiness she had seen in him then, but it was something else—anger? frustration?— that now seeped out from behind his carefully controlled exterior.

"Camden. Come in." Del stepped back to allow him entry and took his hat and greatcoat as he passed.

He shook his head and ran a hand through his hair, causing droplets of rainwater to fly off him.

"Let me get you a drink." She led the way back to the study and poured him a brandy. "Please sit," she said, gesturing to the chair opposite the settee.

They said nothing for a moment, though they watched each other from over the rims of their tumblers. Del wondered what had him so riled. He sat tensely in the chair, his large booted feet set stiffly in front him. He held his brandy tumbler so tightly his knuckles were turning white. His brows were drawn, his jaw tight, his shoulders rigid. Though he always had a serious, reserved look about him, tonight he looked almost—dangerous, as if there was an energy building up within him that threatened to explode. She wanted to ask him what was wrong but she hesitated, as though moving or speaking too suddenly would be the spark that lit his fuse. She didn't fear for herself, of course, but she didn't want to see him self-destruct.

He inhaled, about to speak, but then shook his head and downed the brandy. Wordlessly, Del rose and refilled his glass. And waited.

"Why am I so drawn to you?" he said finally. His voice was strained, as if he were speaking against his will.

Del eyed him, deciding whether to be affronted. Was this what was making him so surly? The fact that there was an attraction between them? What part of it was the worst for him, she wondered, that he was experiencing something he couldn't control, or that he was experiencing it with *her*? By rights, she shouldn't be offended by any of it, for she was just as irritated by her lack of composure when it came to him. Still, she didn't like hearing him speak of it aloud, his expression like that of someone who had eaten something gone rotten weeks before.

"*Are* you drawn to me?" Del asked, deciding to be difficult.

Camden looked at her, his face clearly showing anger, frustration, confusion, and something else, something Del couldn't quite identify. "Yes," he said, gritting his teeth. "In defiance of everything I am, everything I've been told to be—I can't stay away."

"Everything you've been told to be?"

Camden pushed out of his chair as if it had suddenly caught fire. He stalked around the study, looking at Del and then looking away. Many times he stopped, drew in his breath, ready to speak, before letting it out in a frustrated rush and resuming his pacing. Del waited quietly. She would not press him to explain himself. Whatever it was he wanted to say, he needed time before he could tell her.

"I have always done what he asked, behaved as he expected," Camden said finally. "I have obeyed him without question. But in this, I cannot."

Del knew Camden referred to his father, and she could guess what order he was rebelling against. "Your father told you not to see me anymore," she said. She brought her glass to her lips and sipped the brandy, then leveled her gaze at Camden. He nodded, confirming her statement. "And yet here you are, sitting in my study, drinking my brandy," she said.

She wasn't sure yet what she thought about the situation. It was not unexpected, that a father would warn his son away from her, that he would be concerned with her effect on the family's social standing. It *was* unexpected, however, that she should feel such pang of irritation and—hurt from hearing Camden say it.

"Yes, here I am." Camden walked over to the sideboard and distractedly fingered the decanter and glasses. His fingers curled tightly around the neck of the decanter and released, then curled again, as if he were trying to restrain himself from choking it. "When I should be at the shipping office working, or home at my townhouse calculating the quickest way into some society maiden's heart, or even off getting drunk with Farber. I should be anywhere but here."

Suddenly, Camden was at the settee, looming over Del like an angry storm cloud. "Bloody hell, woman, why can't I stay away?" He dropped on his haunches in front of her, searching her face as if it held the answers to his torment.

Del knew she should say something. She should lay a hand gently on his arm and murmur reassurances. Or she should feign outrage and righteous indignation and throw him out of her townhouse with admonishments to never darken her door again, so he would be released from his anguish by the knowledge that now he had no choice but to leave her alone. But she couldn't. Like Camden, she was conflicted, torn between wanting him to go away and never return, and feeling like she would be empty if he ever left her.

Camden took her by the arms and pulled her toward him. His grip was strong and there was tension in his fingers, yet there was strange tenderness about him too. "Is it just me?" he asked, his voice low and husky. "Am I the only one fighting this madness?"

He leaned into her, and Del was warmed by the heat of his body, touched by the energy thrumming just below the surface of his skin. She simultaneously wanted to move closer to him until his warmth enveloped her, and to pull away before she was singed by his fiery restlessness.

"No," Del said, her voice barely a whisper. She brought her hand up to his face, traced the rough outline of his jaw. "I can't stop thinking about you, though it would be better for both of us if I could."

"Bloody hell," Camden said again.

He lifted her off the settee and brought her down to the floor with him. Her nightgown and robe were billowing out around her, pooling around her knees and tangling with Camden's booted legs. He cupped her cheek with one hand, snaked the other arm around her waist and drew her tightly against him. Del felt trembling, but she wasn't sure which one of them was shaking. He brought his face down to hers, his breath hot against her cheek, and Del parted her lips in anticipation. He hesitated for a moment, and Del knew he was still fighting himself, still fighting the attraction between him. Merciless, she threaded her fingers through his hair and brought her lips to his.

Camden made a strangled sound low in his throat, and then some of the tension in him eased, though he didn't become relaxed. That energy was still there, pulsing harder, and Del knew he had given into it and would fight it no longer. He kissed her, hard, like a man long denied of sustenance finally getting his fill.

It was as if all her mental faculties had left Del. Normally in such situations, she felt little and thought much—touch him *here*, make a hungry noise *now*, don't forget to pant heavily as if overcome with desire. All of it to create the illusion that she returned her lover's ardor, experienced the same sexual passion. Now, here, with Camden, there was no thinking, no illusions, no careful control of her responses.

She had no control of anything.

Her entire body responded to him automatically, from the fullness of her lips to her genuine lack of breath to the wetness between her legs. It startled and scared her, that her body had overtaken her mind, that she was not carefully orchestrating their every move. In her fear, she wanted to pull back, to demand he leave so she wouldn't have to feel the burgeoning terror of an actual physical and emotional connection with someone.

Camden seemed to sense her hesitation, and he withdrew his lips from hers, though his thumb brushed lightly over her cheek. "Del," he said, and that simple word, gruffly spoken, was her undoing. It was a question, an answer, a plea, and a pledge. It was infused with both an anguished longing that said he wanted everything from her, and a solemn promise that he would never take what she couldn't give. It told her he was filled with a yearning for her he could barely contain, but that if she said the word, he would muster up an inhuman strength and walk away. It wasn't just about what he wanted and what Del could give him. She could see he would do nothing unless she wanted it too.

"Camden," she breathed, leaning into him. She pushed gently until he was lying on his back, and then she followed him down. He wrapped his arms around her and kissed her again. She pressed her hips into him, his hardness pressing back.

Camden's hands were on her, tentatively at first. They were warm and firm on her back, and when they started to drift lower, he brought them back up to her waist. It was if he was afraid—of what he would do to her, or she to him, Del couldn't tell. She straddled him, tugged at his cravat. Now that she had allowed herself to respond to him, she wanted all barriers between them gone. She rocked her hips against him until he growled. In a sudden explosion of movement, Camden rolled over, one arm under her back so she wouldn't slam against the floor, the other arm holding some of his weight off her.

He drew back slightly and stared at her. Del saw there was much going on behind his eyes, eyes that were heavy-lidded and hazy with passion and trepidation. She wondered what it was he would say to her, but when she parted her lips to speak, he exhaled roughly and covered her mouth with his. She moved restlessly against him. She was mindless, ungoverned, free. She *wanted* this, not as a business transaction or a means to an end or a tool to support herself. She wanted Camden's lips crushing against hers, wanted his hands on her, wanted to feel him, fill her senses with him, connect with him on every level. This kind of wanting was completely foreign to her, and it both excited and terrified her.

"My God, Del, I don't—I can't—bloody hell—"

"What is it, Camden?"

"I don't—I don't even know. You—I can't think properly around you. You're driving me mad."

He sank into her, letting her feel more of his weight upon her. He was hard everywhere, from the lean muscles of his arms, flexed and straining against his coat, to his thighs on either side of hers, pinning her in place, to his stiff cock where he pushed his hips into hers. She moaned and grabbed his waist, trying to pull him closer, though it was not physically possible to be any nearer to her. Every part of her was nothing more than sensation and reaction. Shivers ran through her and gooseflesh rose on her skin wherever Camden touched her. Her nipples were taut and so sensitive that the slightest brush of her silk nightgown against them brought her a touch of pain of the most pleasurable kind. Between her legs, she was engorged and wet, though bereft with the emptiness of not having him inside her. She pulled at him, at his hair to bring him closer to her, tilting his head so she could nip at his neck. At his clothes, trying to pull his coat off him while keeping him pressed against her. At his thighs, loving the feel of his limbs tangled with hers.

He let her tug at him for a moment, and then, as if emboldened by her passion, he finally found the confidence to take the lead. He ran his fingers through her hair and gently pulled her head back until her neck was exposed before him. He leaned in and pressed his lips to the sensitive skin just below her ear, and then to the hollow of her throat, and then along the plunging neckline of her nightgown. She sucked in her breath from the raw pleasure of it and had to consciously remind herself to let it out again. He reached between them and undid the ties of her robe, pulled the fabric away from her body, and tugged at the silk of her nightgown. She wanted it off, all of it, her clothes and his so she could feel his naked skin against hers and be tormented by the sweetness of it.

"Tell me what you want," Camden breathed against her ear. "Tell me what to do."

Any last thread of self-control Del may have been clinging to was obliterated by Camden's request. He wanted to please her, cared about what she wanted and thought and needed. It was more than anyone had ever done for her, and she scarcely knew how to respond.

"I want *you*," she said simply.

Camden looked at her and smiled. He was about to kiss her again when Del put a hand lightly on his chest, stopping him.

"What is it?" he said, concern and confusion showing plainly on his face.

"Someone's at the door," Del replied, inclining her head at the faint knocking sound.

"Ignore it," Camden said. He leaned down to kiss her again, and she would have forgotten all about the person at the door except the knocking became more insistent until Del was worried the visitor would stand outside until he beat the door down.

She nudged Camden off her, and he immediately moved back. "I'll just get rid of whoever it is," she said, "and then I'll return." She licked her lips as she looked at him, disheveled and rumpled and maddeningly enticing.

"Hurry," he said, taking her hand and kissing it before helping her to her feet. He took her face in both hands and kissed her again, as if loath to let her go.

Del smiled and backed away from him reluctantly, slowly disentangling from him. She drew her robe around her and retied it as she walked through the foyer to the front door. She tried to smooth her hair and put herself to rights, but she knew without looking in a mirror that her appearance reflected what she was—kissed senseless and nearly, though disappointingly not completely, ravished.

She opened the door, ready to quickly dispatch whomever it was at her doorstep, but the door swung wide open and a black-clad figure pushed past her.

"Ashe." Del's heart began to beat quickly and heavily.

Lord Ashe stood in her foyer, rain dripping from his hat and topcoat and forming puddles on her floor. His brows were knit together in anger, his jawline was rough with uncharacteristic stubble, and his eyes had the rheumy look of someone who had been drinking heavily. Del shut the door, both to prevent the wind-whipped rain from gusting into her house and to give her a moment to turn away from Ashe and gather her wits.

"It's not a good time," she said as the door clicked into place and she turned back to him. She spoke calmly and softly, as if speaking to wild horse that was terrified and furious and ready to bolt.

Ashe's expression darkened yet more. "When *will* it be a good time?" he snapped. "It hasn't been a good time for nigh on a month now."

"I'm not sure, I—"

Ashe stomped to her and grabbed her arm roughly, cutting off the rest of her response.

"Unhand me," Del said through gritted teeth. "I will not allow you to enter my home and handle me in such a manner."

"And *I* will not allow you deny me any longer." Ashe squeezed her arm and shook her slightly. "We have an agreement. One I pay you handsomely for. I am not in the habit of throwing away coin and not receiving my due."

"Ashe," Del said, and though she tried to make it a warning, she was dismayed to hear just how much fear was breaking through in her voice. She knew what Ashe was capable of. She'd seen him erupt in anger and lash out at whomever he believed had slighted him. "You must leave. Now."

Ashe propelled Del forward until she was pushed against the gilt-framed mirror that hung on the opposite wall of the foyer. He leaned down to her, his face inches from hers, and she could smell the odor of stale alcohol on his breath. "I do not pay you to give me orders, bitch," he snarled. "I pay you to shut up and take it."

Del began to shake, from both fear and fury. Though she usually tried to preserve a cool, unfeeling detachment from any man, allowing herself neither positive nor negative emotions toward them, she hated Ashe in that moment. Hated that he had burst into her house when she wanted no visitors, hated that he remained when she'd ordered him to leave, hated that he had brought up the subject of payment to remind her that he was a wealthy and powerful man and she was just a whore. She should have terminated their arrangement months ago when signs of his temper had first started to appear.

"Leave now," she repeated.

"Do *not* dare to issue commands to me!" Ashe punctuated his statement by slamming her harder into the mirror, and Del couldn't stop herself from crying out as she hit the glass.

"I believe the lady wishes you gone."

Camden stood just inside the foyer from the hallway leading off to the study, though Del scarcely recognized him. He was stiff and tense, which was normal for him, yes, but now there was a thread of something else running through him. Del had seen him trying to keep himself in check before, in their first few meetings when he tried to observe the proper social niceties in the face of an entirely not-proper situation. She had seen him frustrated tonight, when she could sense the anger and irritation in him that almost boiled over. She had thought there was a hint of danger in him earlier, but now she could see what real danger looked like.

He had spoken calmly to Ashe and there was nothing particularly threatening about his words or even outwardly intimidating about his tone, but still there was something in him that made Del realize how much she had been underestimating Camden. It was there in his stance, how every muscle seemed tense, not with reservation or an attempt at propriety but with righteous power barely leashed. It was in his eyes, watching Ashe; in his clenched fists, promising swift retribution should Ashe make a move toward him.

"Unhand her," Camden said, his voice so steady and even it sent a shiver through Del.

Ashe reddened, furious, and his hands tightened around Del's arms. "Who do you think you are, whelp?" He turned back to

Del. "Is this why you won't see me? You've been too busy letting this lad stuff you?"

Del realized Ashe didn't understand the truth of the situation. He looked at Camden and saw merely a young man, barely out of boyhood. He didn't know Camden well enough to see beyond that to what lay beneath. Even if he had perceived Camden as a physical threat, Del knew Ashe expected his superior social station to inoculate him from any harm. As an earl, it would be unthinkable for anyone—especially a young, common, untitled man—to lay hands upon him. But Del could see what Ashe could not, that Camden was prepared to do the unthinkable to protect her.

"Unhand her," Camden repeated.

Ashe pressed Del into the mirror again before pushing away from her and turning to fully face Camden. "Who are you to order me about?" He took a few steps toward Camden. "None of this concerns you, boy, and it's time for you to leave."

Camden walked forward, bridging the distance between the men. "I will not ask you again to remove yourself from this house and leave the lady be."

Camden glared at Ashe, his expression dark and malevolent, and it seemed to Del as though he *wanted* Ashe to refuse him, wanted an excuse to finally loosen the rigid hold he had on himself and let his baser nature overtake him. But once again, Ashe couldn't or wouldn't see what danger Camden held for him

"Lady?" Ashe sneered, looking around the room in an exaggerated manner. "I see no lady. I see naught but a filthy whore and whiny puppy sniffing after her like she's a bitch in heat. A pup that ought to mind his words when speaking to his betters. Now you—"

Camden cut him off with an open-handed slap across the cheek. It was an action a father would make against an impertinent child, or a cruel man would make against a hysterical woman.

For Camden to do it to Lord Ashe was the ultimate insult, far worse than any punch, and Del knew he had done it to inflict the maximum amount of disrespect and degradation possible.

"You goddamn bloody whoreson!" Ashe yelled as he staggered back. "I will ruin you! I will see to it you can never show your face in respectable society again! You and that pathetic social-climber you call a father. That's right, I know who you are, Camden. You're nothing."

Camden stood still through Ashe's tirade, showing nothing resembling fear or concern. When Ashe finally recovered from the shock of being slapped and lunged at Camden, Camden simply cocked his fist back and punched Ashe with such force he went sprawling across the floor.

Del gasped and cried out Camden's name. She wanted to run to him but she was rooted to the floor by the sheer improbability of the scene before her.

Camden went and leaned over Ashe, still lying crumpled on the floor, and grabbed a fistful of his lapel. "You will do nothing of the sort," Camden said, his voice finally reflecting his full power and fury. "You will leave this house and never return. You are never to interfere with this lady in any manner ever again, and you will leave me and my family alone."

"You—I will—how dare—" Ashe sputtered.

"What do you think will happen if 'respectable society' learns the truth of your circumstances? If they knew exactly how you obtained your title and exactly how close you are to losing it? What will you do if my father decides to call in your debts? You know you can't pay and then he will be forced to take possession of your properties he holds title to as collateral."

"What? How did you—I'm not—"

Camden hauled Ashe to his feet. "You think my father loans money to people without first knowing everything about them? You think he doesn't dig up every last scrap of truth, rumor, and innuendo against everyone he can? You think he wouldn't seek any and all leverage against people who could someday assist him in his goals? You think I'm not privy to what he's uncovered? You are an even greater fool than you appear and I have grown tired of you." Camden dragged Ashe to the door, and Ashe, out of drunkenness or surprise or fear or some combination of the three, didn't struggle against him. "Leave," Camden said as he opened the door and pushed Ashe out into the rain. Closing the door, he leaned into it for a moment, breathing heavily as if trying to gather himself.

Del still stood pressed into mirror, her breath coming out in ragged gasps. Camden turned to her and his eyes locked on hers. Once again, she was surprised by what she saw in his face. Gone was any violence or anger or fury. His countenance now reflected only concern and tenderness.

Camden walked slowly toward her. "Del—" he said, and it sounded like an apology.

"What are we doing?" Del whispered.

Camden stopped. "What do you mean?"

"This—us—it can't work."

Camden looked stricken, as if Del had slapped him as mercilessly and cruelly as he had Ashe. He was about to say something, perhaps tell Del she was wrong, but then he closed his mouth and gave a resigned nod. He stared at her silently for a moment more.

The longer he looked at her, the more Del's resolve waivered. She wished he would say something to her, argue with her, take her into his arms and tell her she was being a fool. She wished she had the courage to do any of those things to him.

In the end, he only nodded again and then disappeared out her door and into the cold rain.

Chapter Six

Camden leaned over the billiard table, the heated slate beneath the green baize warming his fingers. He moved the cue back and forth through his left hand as he lined up the shot, calculating the angles and ball speed needed to score his count. He drew the cue back and struck his ball, and then watched as it hit and then bounced off Wittingham's cue ball and rebounded into the red object ball. He empathized with the balls as they scattered and rolled. Like them, Camden felt as though he were being pushed through life, struck from behind, propelled by choices and demands not of his own making, bumped off course by the various obstacles in his way. As though he had no control over the path his life was taking and at any moment he could veer helplessly into an entirely different direction.

"Nice shot," Wittingham said. "Even as distracted as you are, you can still beat me at carom. Must be the advantage of playing on your own table."

Camden shrugged as he walked to the sideboard to fetch his brandy, deciding to ignore Wittingham's mention of his distraction. He leaned against the wall to watch Wittingham take his turn. He had hoped he would be successful in hiding his mood from his friends. He had begged off spending the evening with Farber and Hollingsworth, claiming work but really just unable to endure the prospect of feigning any joviality or enthusiasm for a night spent drinking and gambling. Wittingham hadn't been as easy to turn away; unlike Camden's other friends, Wittingham paid attention to matters beyond his own quest for entertainment, and had insisted upon spending the evening with Camden at his townhouse.

Clearly, Wittingham had sensed something was occupying Camden beyond his usual frustration with his father and the shipping company, and was now trying to get Camden to talk about it. Camden didn't want to talk about what was bothering him, however. He didn't want to talk about it, think about it, didn't want to have the goddamn images running through his mind. He didn't want to relive his shame, how he had let his anger consume him, how he had behaved in such an uncouth, violent manner. He hadn't been able to help it. When he saw Ashe handling Del so roughly, when she had cried out in fear or pain or both when the man had pushed her into the mirror—the edges of his vision had gone red and for a moment he had thought himself capable of actual murder.

Camden especially didn't want to think about what happened after, how Del had looked at him, anguish written clearly on her face as she had told him it wouldn't work, that he had essentially ruined any chance of anything happening between them. He had spent his life keeping himself firmly under control in order to achieve everything his father wanted from life, and now that there was something he actually wanted for himself, he had behaved the brute and driven Del away.

Camden wasn't about to tell Wittingham any of it, though, no matter how subtly his friend pushed for answers. He wasn't about to admit his faults out loud, wasn't going to explain how he had felt when Del looked at him, wasn't going to say how the whole thing ate at him now.

Camden heard the snap of the cue against ball and looked up from his brandy to follow Wittingham's shot. His cue ball hit the object ball but swung wide of Camden's ball. No count.

"Damn," Wittingham said. "You'd think I was the one moping about over a woman, the way I'm playing."

Camden jerked his head from the table toward his friend. "How did you know?" he said before he could stop himself.

Wittingham gave a wry smile. "I didn't, exactly. I just see things and hear things. Things like my good, stoic friend Camden stepping out several times with some blonde beauty. I assumed there must be some attraction there. And given your rather wretched moroseness the past several days, I surmised the state of the attraction to be tattered at the moment, and perhaps not from your desire that it be thus." Wittingham brushed past Camden as he went to pick up his own drink. "And now you've just confirmed it for me." He gulped his brandy and then eyed Camden, his expression all feigned innocence.

Damn Wittingham and his way of extracting information. He should work for the bloody government.

"So tell me, Camden, who is she and what have you done to muck it up with her?"

Camden gritted his teeth. He resolutely avoided looking at Wittingham as he walked to the carom table to take his turn. He bent over the table and cleared his mind. He brushed aside the memories of Ashe, red-faced, belligerent, and threatening. He refused to think of how he, Camden, had been so angry, how the rage had bubbled so close to the surface, that he could have beaten Ashe to death on Del's foyer floor and been happy to have done it. He wiped his mind of how Del had looked, fear and anger and frustration and helplessness all tangled together on her face. So achingly beautiful, so strong and vulnerable all at the same time.

He steadied his hands and slowed his breathing. The only thing he saw was the carom table before him, the only thing he felt was the warmth from the heated slate, the only thing he heard was the crack of the balls hitting each other.

Another count scored.

Camden was reassured. He was in control. He was still able to rein in any wayward thoughts or unruly emotions and focus solely on the task in front him. It calmed him, the knowledge that he still had himself on a tight leash.

Camden glanced at Wittingham as he backed away from the table. He consciously schooled his features into an expression of bland impassivity. "There's no one," he said. "Just the usual tiredness from work."

Wittingham arched a brow. He stared at Camden silently, making no move to the billiards table to take his turn.

Camden grew uncomfortable. "What?" he said defensively.

"I am merely trying to decide whether to allow you your obfuscation, or if I should call you on it."

"I'm not obfuscating," Camden insisted, though he knew he did not sound convincing.

"So we're going with 'tiredness from work' then, are we?" Wittingham tossed his cue stick on the table, surrendering to Camden's insurmountable lead. "Perhaps you ought to take a holiday from work, go have some fun."

Camden made a snorting sound, as if Wittingham's suggestion was the most absurd thing he had ever heard. "My father would never allow it."

Wittingham leaned against the billiard table and drained his brandy glass. He was as impeccably dressed as ever, his waistcoat pristine, his cravat expertly tied in a complicated knot, his expression smooth and mostly aloof with just the slightest hint of his usual snobbish disdain for life in general. It was only because Camden knew him so well that he could identify the signs of slightly drunken and somewhat exasperated concern. Wittingham's eyes were slightly red-rimmed, his *S*'s faintly sibilant, his posture just a touch less than impeccable, and he looked like he wanted to grab Camden by the shoulders and shake him. He leaned in a bit, and for a moment Camden was afraid he would do just that.

"Have you ever considered," Wittingham said as he walked to the sideboard to pour himself another brandy, "telling your father to sod off?"

"Wittingham, really," Camden said with all the careful patience of a reassuring adult speaking to an outrageously fanciful child—or to a man gone regrettably insane. "Stop talking nonsense and—"

"No, I mean it. Tell your father exactly where he can stuff his stupid company and his never-ending demands and go off on a much-needed, well-deserved, and long-delayed holiday."

Camden was about to tell Wittingham exactly why that was such a ridiculous suggestion when he realized he wasn't sure what to even say. Why *shouldn't* he have a holiday? He had been working non-stop for almost two months, never taking a full day off, and rarely even taking the evening off. His father would never approve, of course, but perhaps it *was* time to stand up to his father. He had defied him once, when he went to see Del, and the skies hadn't fallen, nor had the ground swallowed him up for his impertinence.

Except —

He *had* lost his control, he had let his anger swell up and overtake him, and the only thing worse than all that was the fact he had done it in front of Del. She had seen his basest, most ungoverned self. And then she had looked at him and told him it wouldn't work; he didn't deserve to be around her.

In the end, his father had been right: lose your self-control and you lose everything.

So, no, Camden would not be telling his father to sod off or stuff it or whatever other ill-advised imperative Wittingham could come up with. He needed to pacify his father right now, not provoke him. And he needed to regain his discipline, not entertain fanciful notions of taking off on holiday in a fit of petulant rebellion. He most certainly did not need to waste his time pining over a doomed relationship like some Shakespearean star-crossed lover.

Camden realized he would gain nothing by arguing with Wittingham, however. The man, for all his haughty priggishness, was a stalwart friend and an unrelenting interrogator, and Camden knew he would not let up until Camden admitted the error of his ways.

"Perhaps you are right," Camden said, pleased that he sounded convincing. "Perhaps I should take some time away from work, go on a holiday. I've certainly earned it."

"Finally you are talking sense, man," Wittingham said. "Come, let's start your holiday now. I'm sure Farber and Hollsworth haven't lost all their money or passed out yet, surely we can catch up with them."

"Not tonight, Wittingham, I'm exhausted from—"

"Eh, no. No excuses," Wittingham said. He took Camden by the arm and propelled him from the room, grabbing their coats and hats on the way out. "Tonight, you will have fun in spite of yourself."

Chapter Seven

Del tightened the reins as Liath snorted and threw her head, the flighty horse startled and peeved by the sound of snapping twigs and crunching leaves beneath her hooves. Del shifted and pulled her riding habit down to more fully cover her leg. She cursed the necessity of wearing heavy skirts and perching in the awkwardly balanced sidesaddle. Oh, to be able to wear breeches and sit astride the horse, so she wouldn't feel at every moment as though she were about to pitch head first into the dirt.

Del glanced at her pocket watch. She had been riding for nearly an hour, and must be close to the pond where she was supposed to meet Jane, but she could see no sign of it. Finally, after several more minutes, she spotted a copse of trees nestled in a shallow valley, and she knew the pond was just ahead.

Goodness, Jane had told her the pond was secluded, but this seemed a bit extreme. There was nothing else in view, no house or cottage or barn or road, just rolling hills and quietly grazing sheep.

Liath snorted again and sidestepped, the sudden shift in balance nearly throwing Del from the saddle. They had entered the copse, and the horse clearly resented each *thwap* and scratch from the low-hanging branches.

"Steady, girl," Del said as she gently stroked Liath's neck. "We are almost to the pond and the indignity will soon pass."

Del scanned the area, looking for Jane. When her friend had suggested the picnic, Del had tried to beg off, preferring to be glum and morose in the privacy of her own home, but Jane had been insistent. *You need to get out*, Jane had told her. *Fresh air and cold water will set you back to rights.* Del had tried to protest that there was nothing about her that needed righting, but Jane had not let it go. Now, here in the valley, with the sun sparkling off the ripples of the pond and the breeze gently rustling the autumn-touched trees, Del was glad she had finally agreed to the picnic. She did need this, she realized. She had been shut up in her townhouse, alone, for weeks, pretending she was merely feeling a bit under the weather and needed some time to rest. While she had been able to convince herself of that for the first few days, it was becoming increasingly difficult to pretend, to herself or anyone else—particularly Jane—that she would regain her usual demeanor anytime soon. A day spent outside of London, lazing near the water, eating and napping and perhaps swimming, was exactly what she needed.

Del dismounted and wrapped the reins around a low-hanging branch, giving Liath enough lead to graze. She smoothed her hair and skirts, her body and clothes both stiff and rumpled from the ride. It appeared Jane had not yet arrived, and Del was thankful for the time alone to stretch her legs and revel in the quiet solitude. She loved Jane, but once her friend arrived it would be all excited chatter and gentle ribbing, with no restful silence to be found.

Liath's whinny drew Del's attention to the trees behind her, where the rustle and snap of the trees and the jangle of a horse's bit told Del that Jane had arrived. She began to call out a greeting but the words died on her lips.

The horse that emerged from the trees carried not Jane, but Camden.

He wore no hat, coat, or cravat, and his linen shirt was open at the throat, exposing a triangle of hard chest. Like the other time she had seen him astride a horse, his mien was comfortable, carefree, almost cheerful. It transformed him, this happiness, into something Del barely recognized. He didn't look like the staid and serious young man of her acquaintance. This Camden looked wild, his blond hair blowing in ungoverned waves around his tanned face, flushed from exercising in the fresh air. His hands were ungloved, his fingers rough and strong around the reins. His sleeves were rolled up to the elbow, and Del watched the muscles in his arms flex and contract as he guided his horse through the brush. She had seen such a thing described in every gothic romance novel she had read—how the hero was all untamed raw power and animalistic grace. The trite phrases always made her groan when read in print, but seeing the actual physical embodiment of them sent a shiver of excitement through her.

She was so enthralled with watching Camden that she almost forgot to wonder what he was doing at the pond. It was too remote and removed from London for it to be mere happenstance that they would both appear here at the same time. How did he know she would be there? Why had he decided to confront her? She was about to call out to him, demand answers, but the startled and confused look on his face stopped her. He was as surprised as she to find himself in the present company.

"De—Miss Beaumont," Camden said as he dismounted.

"Mr. Camden," Del replied, trying to sound nonchalant. It jolted her that the man she had been working so hard to erase from her memory should now be standing before her.

Camden looked around, as if he expected someone else to be hiding in the trees.

"You look confused," Del said.

Camden cleared his throat. "I am a bit. I hadn't expected to find anyone besides Wittingham here."

"Wittingham is a friend of yours, I suppose?"

"Yes."

"You were to meet him here for a picnic?" Del asked, gesturing to the blanket rolled up behind his saddle and the leather satchel overflowing with food he carried in his hand.

"Yes."

Del's cheeks grew warm as she unraveled the conspiracy. "Let me guess, this Wittingham noticed you've been out of sorts lately and suggested a ride into the countryside would do wonders to improve your foul mood. He then gave you directions to an unnecessarily far-flung and secluded location and told you he would meet you there today at noon."

"How did you know?" Camden asked.

"Because Jane did the same to me."

"So we've been set up."

"It appears so."

Camden laughed, but the burst of merriment didn't completely supplant the dark expression on his face. "I can only imagine how this came about."

Del shrugged. "Perhaps Wittingham and Jane encountered each other somewhere and, after discovering how we are all mutually acquainted, hatched this outrageous scheme. It's of little consequence how it actually happened, for the result is the same regardless."

"Damn you, Wittingham," he muttered, as if his absent, scheming friend could hear him in London. "You can never leave well enough alone." He turned from Del to his horse and then back again, as if he couldn't decide whether to stay or go.

Del could empathize.

"I'm sorry for the intrusion, Miss Beaumont. I assure you I had no idea what Wittingham was up to."

Camden gathered the reins, and Del knew he was about to remount his stallion. She should let him go, let him ride back to London and out of her life and then finally she would be free of him and the turmoil he caused. But once again, she found herself unable to do it.

"Camden, wait," she said, the words spoken before she could stop herself. "There is no reason to leave just yet. Let the horse rest, and we may as well make good use of the food you've brought, if you don't mind sharing."

Camden looked at her, and Del worried he would refuse her. She hadn't thought of that when she'd spoken, that he would want nothing to do with her after she had so inelegantly rejected him. Perhaps it would be for the best if he took the decision out of her hands and refused any further contact. Perhaps then she could stop fighting herself over him and truly move on.

He reached for his saddle, and though Del knew she should be relieved that he was leaving, she couldn't tamp down the twinge of pain and regret that surged through her. She closed her eyes, as if watching him go would be unbearable, but when she opened them, he was not gone. Instead, he had taken the blanket and spread it out on the ground and was now unpacking the satchel of food.

Del moved to the blanket and sat down. She broke off pieces of bread and cut slices of cheese, and otherwise busied herself readying their plates of food.

"I've only brought whisky," Camden said, holding up the cut-glass bottle of brown liquid. "I was expecting Wittingham," he added by way of explanation for not having a more female-appropriate libation.

"I could use a bit of whisky," Del said as she held up one of the tumblers. Camden obliged in pouring her a draught.

The food unwrapped, cut, sliced, and plated, they ate in a slightly awkward, although mostly companionable, silence. Del sipped the whisky, and soon heady warmth traveled through her body and her limbs began to tingle. She relaxed, and the running dialogue she had been having in her head for weeks—about desire versus practicality and the illusion of carefree independence versus the realities of life—finally quieted. She leaned back on her hands and stretched her legs in front of her, closing her eyes to listen to the sounds of the countryside. She hadn't done this since childhood, sat on a blanket on the ground in the sunshine and let herself just be in the moment.

She opened her eyes to find Camden watching her. She couldn't interpret the look on his face, whether he thought her silly or childish or something else. She felt uncomfortably exposed, like a specimen under a microscope. The way he looked at her, it was as if he could see past her artfully composed façade into her raw, naked core. For the first time, it was if another person truly *saw* her. It made her want to run and hide. It made her want to stay and bare herself yet more to him. She still didn't know which impulse would prevail.

"I admit to being surprised you wanted to stay and eat with me," Camden said. He looked down at the hunk of bread in his hand, as if afraid to meet her eye, as if he were embarrassed or contrite.

"Why wouldn't I?"

"Because of—the last time we met. How I behaved—" Camden gulped his whisky.

"What do you mean?"

"With Ashe, when I struck him, when I lost control. I—what you must think of me—"

Del knitted her brows, confused. "I think you were entirely justified in your behavior with Ashe."

Camden's head whipped up, and he looked at her finally. "But your reaction, you told me to leave."

"You think I was upset with you?"

"Weren't you?" Now it was Camden's turn to appear confused.

"No, I wasn't. It wasn't you. It was just—" Del took a deep breath, uncomfortable with the conversation. She was so accustomed to hiding her true thoughts and feelings it was difficult to let herself open up. "You know who I am, what I do." Camden opened his mouth to speak, but Del waved him off. "And all of London does, too. When I'm with you, I tend to forget, but the world never does. It reminded me at the play, when we saw Hutchence, and he looked at me like I was something unpleasant he had just stepped in. And then again, with Ashe—" Del hesitated, losing her nerve.

She was telling him too much, giving him too much, but she couldn't quite stop herself.

"What?" Camden said softly, encouraging her.

"It was just one more reminder of the impossibility of us ever being anything to each other." Del wished the words unsaid as soon as they left her mouth. She had been too bold, all but telling him she wished they could be together. She could see Camden was about to ask her something, but she couldn't bear to hear the question, and so she decided to distract him. "You truly thought I was upset with you?" she asked.

"Well, yes."

"You thought the slightest outburst of emotion would cause me to turn my back on you. You keep a very tight rein on yourself, don't you?"

"An ungoverned man is a weak man."

"I have heard you make similar pronouncements," Del said, "but it never sounds like *you* talking. It's your father who believes such things, isn't it?"

Camden's expression grew cloudy, and Del worried she had pushed him too far, that he would put up a wall between them she would be unable to breach. He looked away from her, watched the ripples of water lap at the rocky edges of the pond. "Yes."

"And do you agree with him?"

"I thought I did. But now—" Camden sighed and shifted his weight, stretching his long legs in front of him on the blanket. "Now I don't know what I think."

"What's changed?"

Camden returned his gaze to Del, his eyes fixed on hers. "You," he said simply, and Del's breathe hitched. "You live your life on your terms, and you don't seem to give a damn what anyone thinks of it. I envy you."

"I've merely followed the only option available to me."

"What do you mean?"

Del bit her lip. Once again, she was having an internal struggle with how much to tell him, how much of herself she could expose. She looked at him, his face showing patience and concern, and she took a deep breath and decided to plunge ahead. "My parents died when I was five," she said, and she had to look away from his expression of empathy and regret before she lost her nerve or broke down sobbing. "It was an illness that took them, and I could do nothing but sit and watch for weeks as they suffered, weakened, and finally—perhaps mercifully—died. I was powerless to do anything for them, to help them or cure them or even mitigate their pain. I could only watch their slow decline and know there was nothing I could do." Del took a sip of whisky, thankful for the sense of warmth and fortification it gave her. "I was sent to live with my mother's sister after. They weren't close, and I had only met her once before. She wasn't a cruel woman, exactly, but she was flighty and selfish and prone to alternating fits of extreme energy and deep melancholy. She had little concern for me beyond the money that came with me for my care, and once that was gone she sent me to live with a distant cousin. That woman *was* cruel and—" Del broke off. She bit the inside of her cheek and pressed the heel of her hand into her mouth to keep from crying.

She silently cursed herself. After all the years that had gone by, after everything she had done to free herself of her past, it could still bubble up and overtake her, making her feel as though she were once again a small, helpless child, alone and bereft and in no more control of her own fate than a feather floating on a strong wind.

"Del, I'm sorry," Camden said, and Del could see he meant it. He wasn't mouthing an empty platitude; she could see it pained him to hear her story.

"After years of being passed around to different relatives, of living in circumstances ranging from merely lonely to actively miserable, I became determined to never depend on another for my well-being. But what could a young girl do to make her own fortunes?"

"Surely marriage or—"

Del scoffed. "I was an orphan with no dowry, no connections, no access to society high or low. I had no means to find a husband of any sort, let alone one who would take as dismal a prospect as I presented. Besides, marriage would have given me no more power over myself than what I had previously. I would have been beholden to my husband, some man I had become tied to for expedience and necessity rather than any kind of affection or desire. I would have had no property, no money, no independence. Marriage would have amounted to trading in one kind of servitude for another. I longed to be free of my bondage, not trade it in for a prettier, more socially acceptable kind."

"And so you did what you had to do, and I cannot fault you for it," Camden said solemnly, and Del could hear in his voice that he truly understood her and did not judge her for her choices.

"Yes," Del said. "I found my independence and made my fortunes the only way I could, and I make no apologies for it."

She wanted to add more, but she wasn't yet able. She didn't know how to tell Camden that lately, since meeting him, she was beginning to question whether she truly possessed the independence and power she had always sought. For as much as she had gained, she was beginning to think she was losing almost as much. She had her own house and her own income, but she had no one close to her to share it with. She was not dependent on anyone else's benevolence to meet her needs, but there was no one with whom she could share her wants and desires. She knew countless people, but no one she could call a true friend, save Jane. She had sex but no intimacy. She conversed for hours at a time with various people, but no one knew who she really was. They knew nothing of her thoughts or feelings, likes or goals.

"I do sometimes miss the closeness a good match could have brought," Del said. It was a deliberately vague statement, but it was all she could give at the moment.

"Indeed," Camden said, and in that one word, Del knew that he had, as he always did, heard beyond her simple statement and understood what she was really trying to convey.

Camden poured them both more whisky. "My father grew up poor," he said, and though it seemed a non sequitur, Del knew he had taken her gift of self-exposure for what it was, and was now returning it in kind. "Grindingly poor. His mother was weak and sickly, and his father was a sot and a bully who drank and gambled away whatever money the family happened to earn. My father would wake up some mornings to find a sibling gone, sold for work or—other unpleasantness." Camden shook his head, as if it were all unspeakable. "He wouldn't really talk about it, just a few comments here and there that hinted at a wretched childhood. He developed an all-encompassing drive to better himself, to create a means to escape his circumstances since none was going to just present itself. And he succeeded. He not only clawed his way out of the dire conditions of his youth, he became massively wealthy. He built a thriving business out of nothing, amassed properties and carriages and all manner of material goods. And he did it on his own, with nothing but sheer determination and stubbornness. It's positively unheard of. But it's not enough for him, he always wants more. Not just more money, but a title, and if not that then at least greater social respectability." Camden shrugged and gulped his whisky. "The thing is, I'm beginning to think it will never be enough. That no matter what wealth or social position he achieves, it won't fill the hole inside him because that's not what he's really seeking."

"And your father has made his goals yours as well, hasn't he?" Del asked.

Camden nodded. "If we are just driven enough, he tells me, disciplined enough, ruthless enough, we can make privileged society accept us as one of their own. But they can sniff it out you know, that he doesn't belong. His accent, his manners, he is like a small child in his father's clothing, trying to pass himself off as man. He only succeeds in looking ridiculous." He gave a weak smile. "He's become increasingly frustrated over the years as his wealth has increased but his social standing remains far below where he thinks it ought to be, and he now thinks it's up to me to secure our social position."

"You don't seem overly concerned with such things, though."

"I'm not, though I don't think my father could even conceive of such a notion. I'm a man of legal age with an immense inheritance poised to take over an enormously successful business, and yet I don't want any of it. I feel no more in control of my life than you did. Independence, freedom, control. I sometimes think it's all an illusion."

"What *do* you want?" Del asked.

Camden seemed surprised at the question, as if no one had ever asked him that before. "What do you mean?"

"If you could go anywhere, do anything, what would it be?"

Camden looked thoughtful. "I'm not even sure."

"Hmmm," Del said, sizing him up. "I could see you breeding horses on a small, quiet farm up north."

"What makes you say that?" Camden looked a bit spooked, as if she had read his thoughts.

"It's the way you look when you ride Sebby, the way you talk to him, handle him. You are usually the most reserved, guarded person I have ever met, but when you are around horses you seem—joyful."

"As I've told you before, horses are so much easier to understand than people. They have no expectations, place no demands—save a clean stall and plenty of food, of course."

Del laughed. "It's more than that, though, isn't it?"

"Yes," Camden said softly, "it is. I'm not sure I can explain it—when I am riding Sebby, I can feel his power and it is simple and pure and raw. It is as close to real freedom I think I will ever get, the feeling that I could gallop away to anywhere, jumping any obstacle in my way." Camden looked down at his hands, flexed as though they were even now holding the reins. "I suppose I sound positively idiotic."

Del laid a hand lightly on his arm. "Not at all. I understand the desire to escape, to leave it all behind."

Camden covered her hand with his and met her eye.

Del's breath caught.

Her surroundings suddenly shrank to include only her and the man sitting beside her. She could hear his breathing, deep and even. She could hear her own pulse in her ears, rushing and slightly erratic. His hand on hers was large and warm and her skin was hot where they touched. It was as though every nerve, every feeling and sensation were concentrated where their hands met.

It was the whisky, Del decided, that made her bold and temptatious. She wanted to lunge at him, to tug at his shirt until it fell away and beg him to do the same to her, until nothing stood between them. She laughed and shook her head, as if she could shake the wanton thoughts from her mind. She began to pull her hand away, but Camden's fingers tightened, stopping her.

"Del." He brought his other hand up to her face, gently rubbed his thumb along her cheek, but he said no more.

She saw the stark wanting on Camden's face, but she also felt his hesitation and knew he was leaving it up to her. If she withdrew from him now, he would let her go, and her life could return to the way it was: simple and predictable and without pesky complications.

It was a lie, though, and she knew it as soon as she thought it. Things would never be simple again. She had met Camden and he had breached all of her defenses and now she was raw and exposed, like a nerve jutting through a bloody, jagged wound. She could go back to London and never see him again, but she wouldn't be the same. The truth was, she didn't want to be without him. It terrified her to think it, however, much less communicate it to him through either word or action.

Leaning into him now would be a declaration, one she couldn't take back.

"Del," Camden said again, and Del could hear the warning in that simple utterance. *Take me or leave me, it is your choice to make, but you must decide now*, he was telling her.

A thousand panicked thoughts raced through her mind, and Del knew she was in danger of being overwhelmed by them. She had to take control of herself, to choose a course of action before he slipped away. She shut off her mind and took a deep breath, like a diver about to plunge into the ocean. "Camden," she said, leaning into him just a bit.

He smiled. She had given him the answer he needed.

Camden brushed a few stray tendrils of her hair from her eyes and then cupped her face with both hands. He stared into her eyes for a moment, gauging her, before leaning in to brush his lips against her forehead. He pulled away slightly and his hands dropped to rest on her arms, and Del knew he would not ask anything more of her.

But *she* wanted so much more.

Now that she had taken the plunge she wanted to go the full depth, and she was not content with a sweet and gentle—but entirely too chaste—kiss to the forehead. She grabbed a fistful of Camden's shirt and pulled him to her. His eyes widened in pleased surprise. He brought a hand to the back of her head, his fingers tangled in her hair, and he pressed his lips to hers. The contact sent waves of heat through her body. She was electrified, entranced, and desperate for more of him. She touched his cheek, ran a thumb along the roughness, reveling in all the tactile sensations he presented.

She pushed into him until he was lying flat on his back, covered by her body, her skirts flowing around them. She kissed him hungrily, and he let her, until she could feel his intensity increase and he rolled over and their positions were reversed. Del clawed at him, greedy and impatient, but he drew away.

"You are so beautiful," Camden said, his voice low and barely audible.

He looked at her as though she were a sacred miracle unfolding before his eyes, and it took her breath away. He didn't see her as lesser, as a merely a vessel for his prurient desire, as a creature who owed it to him to be available for his needs but then should be shamed and discarded because of it. He saw beauty in her, value in her, even redemption and salvation in her. She knew it by the way he touched her, gently and almost reverently. By the way he held her gaze, that simple action telling her he heard her, and saw her, and knew her to be a full and complete—and worthy—person. By the way he defied the orders of his domineering father and the judgment and opprobrium of a disapproving society to be with her.

It wasn't that she needed Camden's approval, that she would demean herself to seek it or change her fundamental being to keep it. It was humbling nonetheless to know he so freely gave it, that he saw beyond her surface, knew her fears and flaws and anxieties, and wanted her for all of it.

"Kiss me," Del demanded, unable to bear the space he had put between their bodies.

She put a hand behind his neck and pulled him down to her. He complied, covering her lips with his and kissing her until she couldn't breathe. She tugged at his shirt until the buttons gave way and the linen fell away from his chest. His skin was a shock of heat in the coolness of the autumn day, and Del pressed into him, letting it envelop her. She ran her hands along his torso, feeling the rise and indentation of each muscle. It sent shivers through her, his heat and hardness, and when he groaned against her neck and his skin rose in gooseflesh beneath her fingers, she knew he was affected too.

His kisses became harder, more urgent and restless. He shifted his weight slightly to one side and ran a hand along her body, down her side and along her leg, and she felt the heat and energy in his touch even though there were still layers of clothing between them. His fingers caught her skirt and he began to pull it up, exposing her legs. The cool air was a shock to her naked skin and it thrilled and excited her. His hands were on her now, his fingers burning trails along her thigh. He kissed her cheek, her neck, and then moved down to the delicate skin along her collarbone. His hands roamed higher up her side and cupped her breast. She moaned and arched her back. His lips were at the neckline of her gown now, and he was tugging at the fabric when he suddenly stopped, whipping his head up. One of the horses had whinnied, and it brought them both back to their surroundings.

"We must stop," Camden said. He was breathing hard, almost panting, and speaking seemed a great strain.

"What is it?" Del asked, confused, her senses jumbled.

He looked at her, effort and regret written plainly on his face. "We must stop now while I can—"

"What's wrong?"

"We—I can't take you here—in the open, like rutting animals."

Del put a hand against his chest, relieved that it was only a sense of innocent modesty that had stopped him. "There is no one about. No house or cottage or village for miles. We are entirely secluded."

"But—here? Outside?"

"Do you not want me?" Del asked with just a hint of teasing in her voice. It was entirely too apparent just how much he wanted her.

"God no, it's not that, it's just—"

Del smiled. She knew this was a struggle for him, to act against tradition and custom and every deeply held notion of propriety. She wanted to see him free himself, if only just once, from the bonds of societal and paternal expectations and give into his own impulses. She wondered how difficult it would be to coax him into it. She thrilled at the notion of finding out.

"We are entirely alone," Del said. She traced lazy circles on his chest, smiling when his breath hitched. "There is no reason for us to stop." She let her fingers drift lower, to move along the waistband of his breeches. His muscles tensed, but he continued to hold himself in check. She stilled her hand. "Is it that you don't want to, or that you think you *shouldn't* want to?" she asked.

"I want to, my God, I want to," he said huskily. "But you—I don't want you to think I'd debase you—"

Del felt a pang at his sweetness, how he was always trying to ensure he didn't hurt her in any manner. He held himself back not because he didn't want it, but because he was concerned about her.

"I don't think that," she said, her hand moving to explore him again. "And right now I'm tired of thinking anything. I want you, Camden. Here. Now."

"I want you too. And I can't fight it anymore."

"Then stop fighting."

Camden exhaled. He reached for her, determinedly, resolutely, as if all his doubt and hesitation had exited with the outrush of breath. One hand was threaded in her hair, the other cupped the full curve of her bottom, pulling her hips to press against his. She pushed his open shirt down his arms until it fell to the ground leaving his torso naked and flexed. He tugged at the laces of her gown, fumbling with her clothes and undergarments until she too was bared to the waist. Her nipples hardened, and Camden stopped his movements and stared at her, as if to fully savor the sight before him.

He cupped one of her breasts, almost timidly at first, as if uncertain how she would react. When she drew in her breath and arched her back, he became emboldened. He brought his lips to her nipple, licked and then gently sucked, sending waves of sensation down her body to pool as heat and wetness between her legs.

"Harder," she panted.

"I don't want to hurt you," he whispered.

"There is sometimes great pleasure in a little pain."

Camden made a strangled sound deep in his throat, as if what she said had impassioned him almost more than he could bear. He let his teeth graze her nipple, and when she moaned, he did it harder.

She let her hands roam freely over his body. Down his heavily-muscled back, over the curve of his firm backside, along the heated skin of his arms and chest. When her fingers brushed against the front of his breeches, he jumped and his cock stiffened yet more in her hand. She eyed him playfully, biting her lip in a hint of merciless seduction. She rubbed him through the fabric of his clothing. Camden moved restlessly against her hand.

Camden had a fistful of her skirts, and he pulled them up until they pooled around her waist. His fingertips ran the length of one of her exposed legs, traced the curve of her calf, moved along the sensitive skin behind her knee, burned a trail up her inner thigh. Del shivered at the sweet torment of it all. He touched her as though he were an isolated man discovering another person for the first time, all giddy excitement mixed with a reverent awe. She didn't think he was actually a virgin—though she could see he wasn't very experienced—just that he acted like this was perhaps the first time it was more than simply satiating a basic physical need. And she finally, fully accepted that it was the same for her. Here, now, with *this* man, with *his* hands and lips and body, it was like the first time for her. The first time she was fully engaged, fully present, with every part of her body and mind.

She moved urgently against him, not sure what she wanted, just knowing she wanted *more*. His hand was still on her thigh, and then he moved it yet higher until he cupped her between her legs. Del was nearly undone right then.

"Tell me what you want," Camden said against her ear.

"Touch me—there—inside—" Del panted.

He ran a finger between the wet lips of her pussy, smiling at Del's gasp. He slipped his finger inside her, and she nearly exploded from the pleasure.

"I need you. Now," Del said. Her hands went to the buttons of his breeches, and soon he was entirely naked.

Camden pulled at her dress, fumbled with her stays, tugged at her layers of clothing until she, too, was completely bare. Del shivered, from the cold air against her skin, from the exquisite pleasure of the contact of their bodies, from the sweet torture of anticipating more. Camden put a hand on her bottom and drew her back to him, covering her with his body, warming her with his heat. He kissed her, his tongue sweeping inside her mouth. Del melted against him.

She was hot and wet, ready for him, and his hard cock pressing against her hips told her he was ready for her too. "Camden please."

The tip of his cock was against her, and he slid it in, slowly and gently at first, until Del put her hands on his backside and pushed his hips to her. His cock slammed home and Del cried out.

"Have I hurt you?" Camden asked immediately, his concern showing plainly on his face.

"No," Del said. He hadn't hurt her. She had no maiden's barrier for him to break, no virgin's fears that caused her to stiffen and balk. But Camden had breached her just the same. He had seen through her every artifice, broken down her defenses and reached into the very core of her. And now there was nothing separating them. It was just Del and Camden and nothing but naked honesty and raw feeling between them. She couldn't pretend with him, couldn't fake her responses or play the role she thought he wanted. It was visceral, primal, and for once, Del reveled in it.

Camden moved inside her, and Del let herself open up to the waves of pleasure. She moved her hips to his rhythm, moaned and panted and clawed at him. She was a mindless being, pure feeling and sensation and response, and she trusted him enough to let him see it. He drove into her again and again, their mutual desire heightening each other's responses. The pressure built up inside Del until it exploded in the most intense orgasm she had ever experienced. Camden's muscles tensed and thrust into her even deeper, and they both cried out as they rode the waves of pleasure together.

Camden collapsed against her, his face buried in her neck, his breathing heavy and irregular. Del, too, felt breathless, and she was stunned to feel the wetness of tears on her cheeks. Camden's breathing soon slowed, and he rolled to his side, taking his weight off her. He snaked an arm around her and pulled her to him, until she was warm and nestled, tangled in his limbs. He brushed his lips against her cheek, drawing back abruptly when he felt her tears.

"Del, what is it? Did I hurt you?" He looked pained, anguished that he might have caused her harm or discomfort.

"No," Del said, smiling. She brought a hand to his chest, and she felt some of the worried tension leave him at her calming gesture.

"Then what is it?"

"I was just—overcome, I suppose," Del said, and when Camden made a noise of cocky male satisfaction, she swatted him gently. "Quite pleased with yourself, aren't you?" she asked.

Camden smiled, but Del could see the uncertainty behind it. "I wasn't sure I would—please you," he said. "Since you have— that is—" He shifted uncomfortably.

"This was like the first time for me," Del said, rescuing him from his embarrassment. "The first time I've wanted it so much, the first time I've so deeply cared for the man I'm with, the first time I've been so completely given myself over to the experience. I can't—I don't know how to explain it."

"I understand what you mean."

"But you've—I mean, you weren't a virgin—" Maybe she had been wrong to think this wasn't his first time.

"No," Camden said, immediately turning bright red. "No, but it's never been like this."

Del nodded. They understood each other completely. She laid her head on his chest, content for the moment to just be held by him. He kissed her lightly on the top of her head. They lay together silently, until the breeze picked up and Del shivered.

"Cold?" Camden asked. He rose and went to Sebby, fetching another blanket from the saddlebag. He returned to her, wrapped them both in the blanket, and hugged her tight, until Del, sated and warm and blissful, began to feel sleepy.

"What happens now?" Camden asked, bringing Del out of her drowse.

"What do you mean?"

"Between us. How do we proceed from here?"

Del felt as though he had dumped her in the pond. She hadn't wanted to think about that right now. She wanted to pretend, for just a bit longer, that the real world wasn't waiting for them back in London.

"I don't know."

Camden's brows furrowed. He opened his mouth to speak, but then closed it, letting out a frustrated breath.

"Camden, what is it?"

"I want you to be with me," he said in a rush, as if the words had tumbled from his mouth of their own volition. "I don't want you to—see—any other men."

"Camden," Del said. She was feeling panicked, at the thought of both giving up all others and embracing the vulnerability of being with just Camden, and at *not* doing that. How could she go back to her former life now that she had been with him, now that she knew what it was like? "I don't know what to do. I—"

Camden rose to his knees, taking Del gently by the arms and bringing her up with him. "I know how much I'm asking of you. I know scared you are of losing your independence." He looked at her with such a determined intensity it made Del tremble. "But I can't bear the thought of you—of not being with you. Not now."

"I can't just give up my life, give up everything."

"I know," Camden said, sounding calmer and resolute. "I know it's too much to ask, that you give up that life. But I want you to make a new one, with me."

"What are you saying, exactly?" Del's heart pounded.

"I love you, Del. Your strength, your confidence, your independence. Your courage makes me want to be brave, to be better." He smoothed her hair from her face and cupped her chin. "I want you to be with me, always. Marry me."

Del's head reeled. She felt like a ship with tattered sails, listing in the wind. "I don't even know how we would go about this, how we would—and your father, Camden, your father would never allow this."

Camden blanched, and Del knew he hadn't thought of that. "I'll tell my father to sod off."

"Oh, Camden." New tears fell down Del's cheeks. She knew it was dangerous to entertain Camden's proposal, to believe she could marry and have children and pretend her past had never happened. But she wanted it, she so badly wanted to be with Camden and tell his father and society and her fears to all just go to hell.

"No, I mean it. Look, I don't know how this will all work, or exactly what to do with about my father. I just know I want to spend the rest of my life figuring it out with you, together. Unless you don't want me." Camden looked worried, as if that had never entered his mind.

Del thought about lying to him, telling him her feelings ran no deeper than close affection, or being outright cruel to him to drive him away forever. She couldn't do it. "No, I—" Del took a deep breath. "I love you, too. I love your honesty and forthrightness, your integrity. From the beginning, you've seen me as a person worthy of respect and affection, and your kindness and loyalty have humbled me. I can't bear the thought of being without you, of continuing to battle the world alone. I want you with me, I need your strength and love."

"Marry me."

Del's breath hitched. "Yes."

Chapter Eight

"You could at least ask me in."

Del blinked at the man standing at her doorstep.

"Blakely," she said. Her tone suggested she was still trying to convince herself he was truly there and not some apparition she had conjured. "Of course. Come in." She stepped back to let him enter, taking his coat, hat, and cane from him once he was inside.

They stood awkwardly in her foyer until Del remembered herself and ushered him to the study.

"I trust you've been well," Blakely said as he sank into the chair.

"I have," she said.

They stared at each other for several seconds, so much to say between them, so little nerve to even start the conversation.

"It has been months since I've seen you," Blakely said, sounding hesitant. He seemed stiff, cautious, like a man carefully picking his way through a field littered with bottomless holes and countless venomous animals.

"I have been—otherwise engaged." Del smoothed her skirts, hoping her bearing and countenance declared her calm and serene, and betrayed none of the roiled emotions she actually felt.

"Yes, I have heard as much," Blakely said. "Our mutual acquaintances have reported seeing you in the company of a certain young man," he added in response to her raised brow.

Del struggled with what to say next. She bristled at the thought of explaining herself, of seeking approval or absolution from anyone. At the same time, she did feel affection for Blakely, and it seemed only right that she give him some sort of explanation for the alienation of her time and attention.

"Who is he?"

Del was conflicted. She wanted to blurt out everything to Blakely, to tell him all there was to know about her and Camden. She wanted to say it out loud, as if speaking his name and declaring her feelings for him would commit their relationship to the ether and erase her fears, doubts, and conflicting feelings. At the same time, she wanted to keep Camden all to herself, to shoo Blakely from her residence so he would never learn Camden's name or what he was to her. She wanted to protect Camden and her feelings for him, to keep him and the real world as far away from each other as possible.

"My God, it's happened, hasn't it?" Blakely looked at her, all shock and incredulousness.

"Whatever do you mean?"

"Your hesitance. The look on your face. Your disappearance these past months. It can only mean one thing."

"I'm sure I have no idea what you are referring to." Del felt nervous, uneasy. She didn't like being so easily read.

"Someone has finally broken through all your carefully laid barriers. He's ignored the sharp and dangerous edges of your defenses and caught you. Someone's finally caught you."

Del laughed, and it sounded hollow even to her. "Really Blakely, you're being awfully melodramatic."

"I have known you for years, my dear, and I have never seen you in such a state." Blakely raised a hand to cut off Del's protestations. "I am happy for you, truly I am. I only ask that you tell me his name. I simply must know who the man is who could succeed where so many others have tried and failed."

"His name is Camden," Del said, feeling scared and giddy all at once.

"Rhys Camden?"

"You know him?"

"Only by reputation. His father is quite the shipping magnate, though it is said the elder Camden lacks the intelligence and social grace of the son. You could hardly do better for yourself. Is it marriage, then?"

"It is." Del battled the urge to cross herself at the utterance to ward off any bad luck her premature confidence might bring. She was sincere in her desire to wed Camden, and she didn't doubt he was as well, but she still hadn't figured out exactly how they would do it. There seemed so many obstacles in front of them: his father, her reticence to relinquish her independence, society's delight in slapping down anyone who might seek happiness outside its preconceived paths set out for its citizens.

Blakely looked slightly bemused, as if he were trying to decide if the conversation were one big jest. "I should challenge him to a duel," he said, and Del wasn't sure he was joking. "I should force him to prove he's worthy of the prize he's captured."

"Oh, Blakely, really."

"Of course I won't, my dear," he said reassuringly. "But really, why does he deserve you? What has he promised you that trumps all I have offered?"

"Besides marriage?" Del asked, and Blakely had the good breeding to redden at her implied admonishment. "He—understands me. He accepts me. He values me—"

"I have always valued you." There was a note of wounded petulance in Blakely's voice.

"He values me independently of what I can do for him," Del said, continuing as if she hadn't been interrupted. "He is intelligent and witty, and there is so much—*life* inside of him, waiting to burst out. He is kind and caring and—and he makes me feel like no one else has ever made me feel. He—"

"Enough," Blakely said, cutting her off. "I do not think I care to hear any further recitation on the charms of Mr. Camden."

"Why Mr. Blakely, could it be you are jealous?" Del felt a twinge of her old feisty playfulness returning.

Blakely looked at her, his gaze heavy. She saw a host of feelings flit across his face. He *was* jealous. Jealous and regretful and perhaps even a bit sad. "I could have been that for you," he said softly. "That and so much more."

"Oh, Blakely," Del said, her tone at once a reassurance and a warning. "Don't. We could never have made each other happy, not in the end. We are too like each other, both too proud, too guarded, too damned *scared*."

Blakely bristled. "I have never been scared of anything. I am offended at the very implication—"

"We are both terrified and you know it. Our surly confidence is nothing more than bluster, and I have only just realized it. We are afraid of letting our guards down. Afraid of loving fully and letting ourselves be loved fully in return. We would hold back from each other, never giving ourselves completely, until it is too late and we're old and bitter and resentful of all the lost opportunities."

"And you think somehow it would be different with Camden?"

"I know it would be. It already is. I don't feel afraid with him. I feel brave and strong and confident. It feels like work with you. With him, it's easy, and the struggle is in staying away."

Blakely's gaze slid away from her, looking past her to the far wall. She could see he was debating whether to argue with her in an attempt to dissuade her from marrying Camden, or to accept what she told him and leave the gracious loser.

"I have always loved you, you know," Del said quietly. "In my way. But it is the love of a sister for a brother, or a close friend for another. It is better we leave it at that, and not pain ourselves thinking it could be more."

Blakely's eyes returned to hers, and Del saw they held the glassy pain of many regrets.

"Please, Blakely." It was a plea he not make things harder for them than it already was.

He looked at her for so long without saying anything that Del had begun to worry he had fallen into some sort of trance. Finally, he nodded, and Del knew he had accepted the state of things, however reluctantly. "I wish you the best," he said, and Del heard the sincerity in his voice. "I hope he truly is deserving of you."

"He is," Del said, her voice steady and confident. She had no doubt he was deserving; it was *her* worthiness she feared was lacking.

"I suppose there is nothing left to say."

"I suppose not."

Blakely gave her one last searching glance before he rose from the chair. Del walked him to the foyer and fetched his things for him. He paused at the door, his expression suggesting he wanted desperately to find the words to convince her to give him another chance. She could see the struggle, how hard it was for Blakely to just let her go. She couldn't be certain what made it so difficult for him, however—whether it was because he truly wanted her or he simply hated coming in second. That doubt made her all the more grateful for Camden and his forthrightness.

"Goodbye, Blakely," Del said. The farewell was simple enough, yet her words contained a thousand meanings. Appreciation for their friendship, recognition of what they once were to each other, regret for the change their relationship must now face, excitement for what the future held for her. Above all, the sternness of her voice implied their time together was completely over. Blakely must leave her now and never return because they could no longer be what they once were.

Blakely searched her face, and then nodded. Del saw he accepted it, however reluctantly. He bowed to her, a stiff, formal gesture that demonstrated his acknowledgment of the new reality, and then he was gone, swallowed up by the black night.

Del sighed as she shut the heavy front door. She sagged against it, as though she were too weak to stand on her own. The encounter with Blakely left her feeling relieved and with a sense of closure, but it also filled her with a certain nervousness. It was in the open now; she had publically declared her affection for Camden and her intention to marry him. It seemed more real now than when she'd accepted his proposal, for now there was another person who could attest to their engagement.

Del returned to the study, where she poured herself a brandy. The sweet liquor fortified her, filled her with a sense of steady calmness.

There was no turning back now. She had admitted it publically.

She loved Camden and was going to marry him. She smiled then, alone in her study. She did love him, and he loved her, and the thought no longer scared her. She would no longer give in to the fear or uncertainty, she decided. She let her excitement and hopefulness wash over her; for once she didn't try to tamp it down or push it away. It wasn't an easy road ahead of them, but she would be walking it with Camden, and that was all that mattered to her.

How strange, she thought, that the prospect of joining herself with another person no longer terrified her. The idea of marrying someone, of tying herself to him and journeying through their lives together, didn't seem like a sacrifice any longer. Marriage to Camden instead felt like a gift, like she was gaining something far more precious than all the riches in the world. It was startling, really, how with the right man, something that she had spent her whole life avoiding suddenly became the one thing she desperately wanted, the thing she wanted more than anything else.

She let her mind wander. She allowed herself to entertain ideas for their wedding. A simple affair, of course, with the emphasis on their joy rather than the observation of ritual and formality. Her imagination drifted to their shared life together following the wedding. They had talked a bit about where to live, and had decided much of it depended on how placable Camden's father decided to be regarding their nuptials. If the elder Camden surprised them by even tolerating—they scarcely dared for outright approval—their union, they had decided to remain in London for the next few years. Camden would continue to work for his father until he could establish himself in his own business and eventually seek financial independence. If his father instead proved intractable in his disapproval, they would have to move away sooner, a riskier option to be sure, but one they had deemed necessary. It didn't matter to Del, however—wherever she was, as long as she was with Camden, she would be home.

Del's thoughts were interrupted by pounding at the front door. She smiled in anticipation. That would be Camden, she thought, coming to see her. She hadn't seen him since yesterday, and she missed him terribly.

It *was* Camden standing on her stoop, and the sight of him caused her to giggle like a schoolgirl. She opened her mouth to greet him, but was cut off when he moved to her abruptly, one arm snaking around her waist and pulling her against him. His other hand was in her hair, turning her face up to him, and he kissed her, long and hard and passionately. Del was thankful his strong arms were around her, for her legs were suddenly weak and she would have collapsed in a puddle on the floor without his support.

She had a brief, clear thought that she was behaving in an absolutely ridiculous manner. Then Camden's tongue swept inside her mouth and the sensations of her body took over, driving every rational idea from her head, and it would be many hours before she could think clearly again.

• • •

Camden propelled Del back into her foyer, kicking the door shut behind him because he couldn't tear himself away from her for the brief second it would have taken to shut the door properly. He kissed her as he moved forward, his lips crushing hers, his tongue sweeping inside her mouth, his hands grabbing fistfuls of her dress and her hair.

Bloody hell, he loved having her in his arms.

She clung to him and Camden could feel her arousal in the way she trembled against him. She tugged at his coat, pushing it off his shoulders and down his arms until it landed in a crumpled heap on the floor.

"My God, I've missed you," Camden said.

Del smiled. "It's only been a day since I've seen you last."

"That is far too long." He kissed her again, hungrily, greedily, like a child trying to eat all of the candy before anyone could stop him.

It was exactly like that, Camden thought. He wanted her constantly, always hungry for the taste her, and no amount of touching or kissing seemed to fill him. Whenever he was with her, he strained to take in as much of her as he could—her scent, her taste, the feel of her next to him. There was so much about her he had yet to discover and he was impatient to know all of it. Their time together always seemed too brief, but Camden suspected he might feel that way no matter how long they were in each other's company. He didn't think it would ever dissipate, the excitement and longing and wonder he felt for her.

Camden lifted her in his arms and she wrapped her legs around his waist. He backed her against the wall, sending pictures and a mirror askew, but neither of them noticed. They pawed at each other, clutching and grasping at clothes and flesh and hair.

"We should move upstairs," Del whispered.

"Yes, we should," Camden said, but he made no move disentangle from her. He couldn't let her go.

Camden set her on her feet and began to undress her, his lips never leaving hers. Soon their clothes were piled on the floor by their feet and they stood naked together. The marble floor was cold against his feet, and it was as though that coolness was the only thing keeping them from bursting into flames. Del's skin was warm everywhere, her nipples taut, and Camden wondered if she would grow so hot she would actually burn him. He would gladly let their passion ignite, would happily let her fire overtake him until he was nothing more than a smoldering pile of ash at her feet.

Camden felt a hunger and neediness for the woman standing before him that would have unnerved him had he still had the presence of mind to reflect on such things. He had lain with a few women, quick and fervent couplings that served to satisfy the needs of their bodies, but he had never known anything like this. Never before had he felt such overwhelming emotions, never had he been so strongly connected to someone. Every time he touched Del it was a revelation, every time his lips brushed hers he was reborn, every time he looked into her face it was as though he were in the presence of the divine. She made him feel simultaneously like the most powerful man in existence and like a weakened boy unable to escape the enthrallment of a siren. How strange to feel the power of a thousand men course through his body but know that should the house start to crumble around them, he lacked the strength to move even the few steps to her door.

He ran his fingers along the heated skin of her arm and felt her tremble at the contact of their bodies. She placed a hand on his chest and smiled when his muscles flexed involuntarily. He couldn't control the way he reacted to her—her slightest touch awakened in him a desperate wanting; her fingertips brushed his skin and he would shake, burning with the need to be inside her.

He kissed her hard, his tongue pushing into her mouth, possessing her. She grabbed at him, her fingernails raking the skin of his back. He put his hands beneath her bottom, his fingers digging into her flesh, and he lifted her up and once again leaned her against the wall. He pressed into her and she pulled him even closer until his hardness pushed against the wetness between her legs. She gasped at the movement. She was ready for him, as he was for her; his arousal so acute it was almost painful, the friction of his cock against her pussy nearly enough to make him explode right then and there.

"My God, I want you inside me," she panted.

It took everything Camden had to withhold himself from her. The heat between them, the arousal, the jolt he felt each time they touched—it made him feel like a mindless bundle of exposed nerves. Nerves that fired with the exquisite torture of not being inside her. He desperately wanted to plunge himself into her wetness and soothe their aching need for each other, but he held back. "Not yet," he said, breathing hard. "I want to enjoy a little more of you."

He moved away from the wall and dropped to his knees, laying her out on the floor. He ran his hand along her body, gazing upon her like a man laying eyes on something sacred. He found her so very, very beautiful that looking at her made his chest constrict painfully and his breathing become ragged and uneven.

Del tried to pull at him, to roll him on top of her, but he caught her hand in his and, threading his fingers through hers, brought her arm up gently over her head, letting her know he wanted more time to explore her body.

His fingertips ran down the sensitive skin of her arm, across her neck, and over her nipple. She sucked in her breath as it hardened. She arched her back, showing him that she wanted more of his touch at her breast, but he teased her by moving on. He slowly made his way down her belly, along the outside of her thigh. He hadn't realized how sensitive different areas of her body were—the inside of her arm, the back of her knee, the hollow of her neck—until his fingers reached them and her body responded with pure, tingling desire.

He was desperate to please her and so he took great satisfaction in her reactions. Every jump and shudder, each moan and cry revealed just how successful he was. When he discovered something she liked, he teased her mercilessly—running a finger along her inner thigh but then withdrawing his hand or bending to lick a nipple quickly before moving on to her neck—until she quivered and moaned. She pleaded with him to sate her incredible need, but he refused, reveling in the knowledge that his touch was having such an effect on her.

He grew bolder with each signal of pleasure she gave him. He brought her nipple into his mouth, sucking gently at first, then harder when she responded feverishly to him. One hand was under her shoulders, holding her to him, and the other was exploring her freely. His hands were on her thighs again, but this time he let them continue the upward journey, until he slid a finger between the heated lips of her pussy. Del gasped and arched her back, clawing at him. The barest tip of his finger was inside her, exploring, while his thumb found the engorged nub of her clitoris. She rocked her hips against him and he knew she was desperate for more of him, knew she was searching for release. Realizing what caused her the most pleasure, he slid his finger in deeper, his thumb pressed harder, and licked her nipple faster and nipped at her with his teeth, and finally, just as she cried she could bear no more of it, she exploded in an intense orgasm against his hand.

Camden watched her as the waves of pleasure lessened and her breathing slowed a little, and he felt both smugly satisfied and a bit in awe of the reactions of her body. Her orgasm had driven his arousal to nearly painful heights and his cock was hard against her thigh. She reached out to touch him, barely taking his cock in her hand, and he drew in a sharp breath as he stiffened. He knew it would take hardly anything to bring him to his own release. Groaning, he put his hand on hers, stopping her.

Del pulled at his shoulders until he was on top of her, his hips pressed against hers. She was wet and ready for him, and he plunged his cock into her in one hard thrust. She wrapped her legs around him, pulling him closer, arching her back and pushing her hips forward to meet him each time he thrust into her. He bent to kiss her, hard, his lips capturing her cries. She clawed at his back, his buttocks, pulling him deeper into her.

The pressure built until Camden knew she was riding the oncoming ripple of another orgasm. Her cries and moans were his undoing, and he groaned as his cock pulsed inside her. They rocked together, locked in wave after wave of pleasure, until they were both spent and breathless. Camden collapsed against her, his strength completely gone. When his senses returned and he realized he was likely crushing Del, he rolled to his side, taking her with him, and held her tightly in his arms.

Camden was still breathing heavily some moments later and he wondered if it would ever return to normal, if he would ever fully recover. Being with Del had changed him. It wasn't just the physical coupling of their bodies—though God knew that was an amazing part of it—it was also the closeness he felt with her, the joy of knowing she was his and he was hers. He felt so happy and fulfilled that he didn't think it would matter if he died right then and there.

He looked at Del lying sleepily against him and he was hit with such a strong wave of absolute joy and contentment, as though he were a pious man staring with rapturous devotion at his salvation, that he thought perhaps he already had.

• • •

Del lay in Camden's arms, satisfied and drowsy, for an untold dozens of minutes. She was spent and sated, utterly convinced she would never again gather the energy to make love, but then

Camden hardened and Del smiled, knowing she could never truly get enough of this man. She was surprised he needed so little time to recover, but then she realized this was just one of the many advantages of sleeping with a man still so young. He was engorged and ready, eager to please her and find his own pleasure in her body, and Del was more than happy to oblige.

He rose from the floor and picked her up, carrying her up the stairs to her bedroom. He laid her out on her bed and they began to explore each other again. Where before it had been fevered and desperate, this second time it was slower and more measured, each touch imbued with meaning, each thrust long and deep. They found release together and then lay exhausted in each other's arms, recovering.

Del laid her head on Camden's chest, listening to his quickened heartbeat, just now beginning to slow. Her own heart beat a heightened tattoo and her breathing was ragged. Despite the coolness of the autumn evening, they were both cloaked in a thin sheen of perspiration. She felt simultaneously languid and energized, as though their lovemaking had depleted her every reserve of hesitation, fear, and self-doubt, but then replaced it with desire, hope, and contentedness. She keenly felt both the loss and the gain.

Camden's arms were around her and he ran his fingers along her back, tracing desultory circles on her skin. His breathing had become deep and even, his heartbeat finally regular, and Del knew he was a man satisfied and sated, about to fall asleep.

"Blakely came to see me this evening." Del wasn't sure why those words had come out; she hadn't meant to engage in any conversation in particular right now, and certainly not one about another man. From the hitch in Camden's breathing, she guessed her statement had taken him by surprise as well.

"Oh?" Camden sounded hesitant, cautious.

Del propped herself up on an elbow so she could look Camden in the face. He was still rubbing her back, and now he was looking at her with guarded curiosity.

"He wanted to know where I've been recently, why I haven't seen him."

"And what did you tell him?" Camden looked concerned, and Del stretched to lightly kiss his check, wanting to assuage his worry.

"I told him the truth. I told him I loved you and we are to marry, and I wouldn't see him again."

"How did he respond?"

"He was—disappointed, I suppose, but he took it well."

"I'm glad you told me," Camden said. Del hadn't realized he had been so tense until she felt him relax.

"I wanted you to know. I don't want there to be anything between us, no lingering doubts or suspicions—"

"I've never doubted you, or anything between us."

"I know," Del said, placing another soothing kiss on his cheek. "But I wanted any old—attachments dealt with just the same. And I feel relieved. I wasn't sure at first how it would go for me, how I would handle leaving my old life behind."

"Are you feeling regrets?" Camden asked. He tensed again, looking vulnerable.

"None. I feel nothing but relief that the past is done and excitement for the future."

Camden smiled, his masculine assuredness firmly back in place. Del snuggled back into his arms, her head on his chest. She listened to the beat of his heart and felt the rise and fall of his breathing.

Del took a deep breath, gathering the courage to ask something that had been weighing heavily on her. "Does it ever bother you?" Del asked, feeling timid and vulnerable. "What I—was."

Camden looked at her wordlessly for a moment, and Del felt her heart sink. Then he took her face in hands and looked deeply into her eyes, as though he wanted to make sure she would not mistake the meaning of his words. "No," he said firmly. "There is nothing about you that could ever 'bother' me. Everything you've done, the choices you've made or been forced to make, has gone into making you what you are now. Your past, your present, our future together, all of it is part of the woman you are, and I love you for all of it. Nothing will ever change that."

Del looked down, overwhelmed by his love and acceptance of her. He put a hand under her chin and nudged her to look at him. "I mean it," he said.

Del nodded and kissed him, relief flooding her. "I love you too," she said.

She laid her head back on his chest, and they relaxed, enjoying the feel of each other.

"Since we are disclosing awkward conversations," Camden said after some time, "I spoke with my father this evening."

Del's breath hitched. "You told him of our engagement? What was his reaction?"

Camden's breathing quickened slightly, almost imperceptibly, but Del still noticed. He didn't answer her immediately. She gathered the sheets around her and sat up. "I take from your silence he did not react positively."

"It wasn't exactly positive, but nor was it overtly negative."

"Will he approve the marriage?"

"I'm not sure," Camden said. "I am as confused as you are," he added quickly, and Del knew her frustrated emotions were showing plainly on her face.

"What did he say, exactly?"

"He said very little, actually. I went into his office and told him I had asked you to marry me. He stared at me, looking not completely surprised, and then said, 'I see.'"

"That's all he said?"

"Yes, at first. He tensed a bit and it seemed as though he wanted to say more, but he did not. I said I knew he had been skeptical of our relationship in the past, but he only needed to see us together, to spend time with you, and he would know how much we loved each other and how *right* this marriage is."

"Do you think he was convinced?" Del asked. Not knowing the elder Camden, she wasn't in a position to interpret his reactions. It frustrated her immensely, that this cruel and overbearing man who did not know her held so much of her happiness in his hands.

Camden reflected on her question for a moment. "I cannot say with certainty. He didn't say outright that he disapproved or would attempt to halt the marriage. But he did not give me his blessing, either. He merely asked—admittedly rather tersely—if I was sure this was what I wanted, and when I told him it was, he said he needed to return to his work and motioned me out of his office."

"What does this mean? Do you think he will not object?"

"I think he just needs time to accustom himself to the idea. He did not become immediately angry, or declare that he forbade our match, or shout, or throw me bodily from his office, so we must conclude he is not outright opposed to our match. In time, he may fully embrace us."

"And if he does not? What will we do if he doesn't consent to our marriage?" Del tried to remain calm, but she heard the note of panic in her voice. Now that she knew, without reservation, what she wanted, now that she had finally admitted to herself what Camden meant to her, she was terrified that outside forces would conspire to keep them apart.

Camden sat up and took her face in his hands. "It wouldn't matter. My father might want to choose my spouse based on who would best serve his aims to move up in society, but I am of age and can marry whom I love. I do not actually need him to approve." He spoke confidently, reassuringly, but Del still heard the barest hint of doubt in his words.

"Could you really do that? Could you really go against your father, risk your livelihood and inheritance?" She knew what this meant to Camden. It was one thing to declare in the abstract that he cared nothing for the financial riches his position in the shipping company afforded, that he would walk away from it all on principle; it was quite another to entertain the cold reality of it. And no matter how complicated and fraught his relationship with his father was, no matter how grievous the man's abuses against his son, Del knew it was no simple matter to defy a parent and potentially fracture the relationship beyond repair.

"You are what matters to me now," Camden said. "Of course I would rather proceed with his blessing, but I will marry you no matter what." He bent down and kissed her forehead. "I will do whatever necessary to ensure we spend the rest of our lives together."

"Even if it means defying your father?"

"No matter what it means."

Del sank back into the bed. Camden followed, gathering her into his arms. They lay together, talking and touching until the first rays of dawn began to lighten Del's bedroom.

"I must go," Camden said reluctantly. "I am expected at the shipping office shortly."

"Stay," Del said.

"I wish I could, but I'm expected at the offices and I'm trying to stay in my father's good graces. I want to speak with him again, as well."

Del gave him a playful pout. She put her hand behind his neck and pulled him to her, kissing him hungrily while she pressed her naked body against his. "Stay," she whispered.

Camden groaned. "Have mercy, woman." He rolled on top of her, supporting his weight with one hand while he slid the other underneath her. He kissed her, hard, and slowly let more of his weight rest upon her.

"I thought you were leaving," Del teased between kisses. Satisfied that she was the victor—she had enticed him into staying—she would magnanimously release him to his duty.

"You are going to be the death of me," Camden said. He leaned down to kiss her again, clearly loath to let her go.

Del pushed lightly against him. "You mustn't be late," she said.

Camden rose from the bed and went to collect his clothes from downstairs. He returned with them heaped in his arms and Del watched as he dressed, admiring the way his naked body moved in the cool light of dawn. His muscles rippled and flexed as he stepped into his trousers, and Del liked the way the fabric clung to his narrow hips. He was all long, lean lines and hard angles, and the mere sight of him sent waves of desire through Del. He glanced at her and gave her a wolfish smile, and Del knew her lust was visible.

Once dressed, Camden knelt on the bed to kiss her goodbye. Del grabbed a fistful of his shirt and contemplated seducing him again.

"See you this evening?" Camden asked.

Del nodded, lips swollen, lids heavy. Camden gave her a look that suggested he too was considering ravishing her again, and Del knew she must shoo him away before they both gave in to temptation.

"Yes, I will see you evening," she said. She pulled him in for one last kiss and then released him, motioning him to hurry out the door. She heard his heavy footsteps going down the stairs, and then heard the front door opening and closing. She was alone and acutely aware of the empty space beside her.

She used to revel in it, that notion of unattached independence. Now she felt bereft.

She rose from the bed and stretched, wondering what she should do with day. She reflected on this as she dressed, how unusual it was to have so many free hours before her and so little sense of obligation in how to fill them. She decided to eat a decadent and leisurely breakfast and then go visit Jane. She had had precious little interaction with her friend in the past few days, and Del missed her fiercely. They had so much to catch up on, with the betrothal and wedding details and the conundrum of Camden's father.

She was padding across the downstairs foyer, dressed but still barefoot, when she heard the clank of the brass knocker on her front door hitting the strike plate.

"Unable to stay away, Camden?" Del asked as she swung the door open.

Neither of the men who stood on her stoop were Camden, however, and Del froze in surprise for a moment when she realized it. They were, in fact, the physical opposites of him, short and squat, with the physiques of a scruffy bulldog. They both had lined, weathered faces sporting hardened expressions, and they looked and moved so much alike Del knew they were brothers, if not twins. Their clothes were simple yet clean and serviceable, but they looked strange and uncomfortable in their outfits, as though they had been forced to look presentable when they would much rather be dirty and unkempt.

"May I help you?" Del asked, politely yet firmly, finally overcoming her shock and finding her voice. Though not exactly fearful, Del was uneasy about the situation. The men, while not overtly hostile, had a sufficiently strange out-of-place aura about them that made Del nervous.

"Adele Beaumont?" one of them asked, though his voice suggested he had no doubts as to her identity.

"Yes?"

"Have a message from George Camden. We come in?" The man's gruff tone of voice added to his use of truncated sentences gave the impression he had little patience for interpersonal communications of the speaking sort.

"I—it's not really a good time. I was just on my way out." Del took a step back, retreating a fraction further into her townhouse. She wasn't sure what kind of message the elder Camden had for her that necessitated sending two men who looked like barely tamed brutes to deliver it, but Del felt, with rising certainty, that it wasn't pleasant. There was still no overt threat, but every instinct Del possessed, honed over years of vulnerability and hardship, told her to dispatch the men from her doorstep immediately.

"Again, it is not a good time. Perhaps I will stop round the shipping offices this afternoon to speak with him, and he can deliver his message himself." She began to close the door on them, and even though she felt justified in heeding her instincts, she couldn't completely squelch the sense of guilt she felt over her horrific manners.

The man who spoke, the apparent leader, stuck his foot in the doorway, preventing its closure. "'fraid not," the leader said, and Del gulped, unease bursting suddenly into full-fledged fear. He pushed the door open in a violent burst, sending her reeling backwards. "Mr. Camden wants it dealt with now." The two men were in her foyer now, and the silent one shut the door behind them.

Del's heart pounded and she felt dizzy. She expected the men to fly at her in a full-blown assault, but they stood where they were, just inside the door.

"What is it you want?" Del took several slow steps back, her mind racing. Were they really sent her by Camden's father, or were they here to rob her? Or did they have more nefarious plots in mind? She tried to tamp down the abject panic; she would be no good to herself if she completely lost her head. "I-I have money, if that's what you're after." She continued to back up until she was pressed up against the mahogany side table at the far end of her foyer.

"Ain't why we're 'ere," Leader said.

"But the Mister didn't say we *couldn't* take an extra nicker or two," the other said. Leader looked annoyed he had spoken.

"I'll go get money," Del said, trying to keep the men calm and appeased.

"Not going nowhere," Leader said as he took a few steps toward her.

Del fumbled her hands along the table behind her, trying to keep her movements discreet, until she felt the smooth, cool hardness of a candlestick. It was large and heavy, and would do considerable damage to any skull it cracked against—at least enough to let Del make her escape, she hoped.

"Not going to 'urt you," Leader said as he continued to move toward her, his actions doing little to assuage her fear. "Mr. Camden just wants to make a few things clear. 'e wants you to stay away from 'is son."

Del's blood was pounding in her ears, and she heard little of what the man was saying. Behind her, she curled her fingers around the candlestick, her sweating palms making the grip difficult.

"Says you got your whore claws into 'im, bewitched 'im, and it's time for you to let 'im go."

He was close to her now, so close she could smell the smoke and liquor and other remnants of a night of who-knows-what kind of debauchery. She knew she couldn't hesitate. She would have to swing the candlestick hard and fast, and if she managed to hit the man squarely on the temple, she might have enough time to run up the stairs and lock herself in her room. She could only hope his brother wouldn't be able to react in time to stop her.

Before she could think anymore about it, she tightened her grip on the candlestick and swung it as hard as she could at the man's head. It connected soundly, hitting his skull with a dull thud while he cried out in surprise and pain. He staggered back, his hand at his temple, and Del could see blood seeping through his fingers. Del stood rooted for the briefest moment before she dropped the candlestick, picked up her skirts, and bolted for the stairs.

"You fuckin' bloody bitch," the man roared as he lunged for her. He caught one of her arms and swung her around. "Fuckin' bitch," he yelled again as he cocked his fist and punched her, snapping her head back. Pain rocked her skull and she saw bursts of light in her cloudy vision. She dropped to her knees, and then collapsed into a disoriented heap on the floor. She couldn't hear or see properly, and she knew she was in danger of losing consciousness. She only dimly sensed the brothers standing over her, arguing.

"Bloody 'ell!"

"Did you kill 'er?"

"No! I don't know!"

"What do we do now? Leave 'er? Jesus, blood's everywhere."

"Most of it's mine."

"An' you always said I was the cock-up."

"Will you shut up? I can't think. Grab 'er."

"What?"

"Grab 'er, we'll take 'er to Mr. Camden. 'e'll know what to do."

Then there were hands on each of her limbs and Del was hoisted up, the movement causing her head to pound even more fiercely and her stomach to roil. She was vaguely aware of the men carrying her out of her townhouse and placing her in a carriage, and then the world went dark and she was aware of nothing more.

Chapter Nine

Del came to consciousness slowly and painfully. Her head was pounding and her mouth felt dry and raspy. She opened her eyes, trying to remember where she was and what had happened. Her vision adjusted to the dim light of the room and she scanned it for any clues to her location. Shelves lined the wall from floor to ceiling and they were crammed with books and ledgers. There were crates in the corner, though she couldn't see what they contained. There were no windows and only one door. Del was sitting in a chair in the middle of the room and her wrists were bound to it by thick rope. She strained against the bindings, but the knots were tight and the rope dug into her skin. Wincing, she relaxed her arms.

She was afraid, very afraid, but she willfully slowed her breathing and tried to calm down. She needed to remember what happened, to figure out where she was and how she could escape. Panicking would do nothing but cloud her mind and worsen her circumstances. She must be calm and logical.

She tried to reconstruct the events leading up to her present predicament. She remembered Camden coming to her in the evening. She remembered him leaving at dawn. She was having difficulty remembering what happened after that. And then her hazy thoughts cleared and she remembered the two men standing at her doorstep, brutish and sinister and full of cryptic warnings. What had they said to her? What had they wanted? Del strained to remember, but it was hard to cut through all the panic—from then and now.

And then it came to her, what they had said. They had a message from Camden's father; he wanted Del away from his son. The elder Camden had actually sent men to her to warn her away from his son, to threaten her, and they had knocked her unconscious and dragged her—here. But where was "here," she wondered.

She looked around the dusty room again.

They were Camden's men. She was in a room full of legers and crates.

She must be at the Camden shipping offices.

She felt slightly calmer now that she could remember what happened and could guess at her location. Still, though, she was trapped with no ready means of escape. She pulled at the ropes again but the heavy bindings only tore at her wrists, breaking skin and causing small droplets of blood to well at the injuries. She would not be able to break free.

Her mind raced with conflicting desires. She wanted to call out to someone, cry for help, but she knew in doing so she ran the risk of alerting the men who had brought her here—men who clearly meant her harm. She wanted to scream and cry in panic, but knew there was absolutely nothing to be gained by such histrionics.

Think, Del, she commanded herself. She scanned the room again, this time slowly and methodically, looking for something— anything—that would help her. She spotted a small table in the corner to her right. It was littered with various things common to an office: papers, writing implements, books and ledgers. The table was too cluttered to clearly make out everything upon it, but it didn't seem entirely improbable that there could be something there to help her, scissors or a letter opener or something. The room was small and the table was only a few feet from her—so tantalizingly close and yet so frustratingly difficult to get to when one was bound to a chair. Her feet were free, at least, and that would have to do.

She tried to move her weight onto her feet, thinking she could shuffle over to the table while still strapped to the chair. The seat of the chair was too deep, however, and she couldn't quite manage it. She gripped the arms of the chair and tried to "hop" it over a few inches. At first she merely bounced impotently in place, but then it finally budged. The chair legs scraped against the wood floor as it moved. The sound seemed deafening to Del in her frightened state. She froze in place, breath held, and strained to pick up the sounds of anyone coming near. After several beats of her pounding heart, she decided no one had heard her and she carried on.

It was a difficult, torturously slow process. Each time she moved the chair, the ropes gouged at her wrists and soon they were bruised and bloody. She was desperately trying to keep quiet, but the chair creaked and scraped against the floor no matter how careful she was. All in all, it was a great effort for minimal gains, and she despaired at ever reaching her goal.

Del had managed to move the chair perhaps a foot closer to the table when she heard footsteps and voices outside the room, drawing nearer. She held still, not moving, not breathing, and prayed a silent entreaty that the men she heard would walk past her door without stopping.

Her heart sank when the footsteps stopped and the voices grew clearer and louder. There were at least two men standing just outside the room.

"What in the bloody hell could you have been thinking, bringing her here?" one of the men barked. Del heard in his voice the barely contained rage. "My instructions to you were clear: get her to leave town as quickly as possible and promise to never contact my son again. At no point did I tell you to lay hands upon her or bring her anywhere near me or my properties."

His son. So it *was* Camden's father who was behind her abduction, and she *was* being held in his shipping office. That simple knowledge had a strange calming effect on Del. The earlier uncertainty had been terrifying.

"I'm sorry, sir, I—"

"I have no use for your inept apologies! It does nothing for me now! Thanks to you and your even more addle-pated savage of a brother, I have a beaten and kidnapped women on my premises." Del could hear the fury building in the elder Mr. Camden's voice and any relief she had felt just moments ago turned into shaking fear. "And because you told her I sent you, I'm implicated in all this. What am I to do with her?" The words were ominous, and Del knew that whatever answer he found for that question spelled doom for her.

"It was an accident, I didn't know what to do—"

The man—Del recognized the voice as the man who had struck her—was cut off in his explanation by a grunt and a thud, and Del guessed he was being slammed into a wall.

"Enough, Murphy," Mr. Camden said, the words coming out in a furious growl. "I've had enough of your excuses, enough of your incompetence. Not another word from you."

There was a moment of silence, a maddening time when Del couldn't tell what the men were doing and what was coming next. Then the doorknob turned and Del knew she was about to come face to face with her tormentor.

She wasn't sure exactly what she expected to walk through the door but it certainly wasn't the slender, impeccably dressed man who entered the room. From what she knew of Mr. Camden, from what she'd heard from his son and from what he'd done to her, she had thought his sinister character would be more readily apparent. As though one could look in his face and see an unfeeling brutality stare back. She wondered if this was worse, if the man's unimposing build and bland features lulled one into a false sense of security that made the inevitable attack that much harsher.

Her attacker—Murphy—trailed behind Mr. Camden. Murphy was the larger man, squarer, more brutish in body and countenance, more immediately intimidating, yet the way he walked behind Mr. Camden, looked at him, responded to him, was deferential to the point of being almost fearful. It unnerved Del yet more.

Neither man said anything to Del. Mr. Camden walked to her, stopping just inches from the chair where she was bound. She could see now the resemblance the man in front of her held to her beloved Camden. It disconcerted her to see the features of someone she loved beyond reason reflected in the face of someone who so clearly meant her harm.

Now that he stood directly in front of her, his true nature was more apparent. She was struck by how much two men who looked alike, who shared the same blood, could be so entirely different. The father was all irritated stiffness and carefully controlled ire where the son was kindness and light affability. Her Camden was also restrained, yes, but unnaturally and imperfectly, and his joyfulness was obvious enough when you knew where to look. She saw none of the son's goodness in his father's eyes, none of his tenderness or understanding or compassion. The elder Camden's mien was cold and uncaring, and he seemed to possess all the human feeling of a wax figure. His were the uncomplicated emotions of a savage animal: anger, frustration, ruthlessness. It saddened Del to know that her Camden had once been a small and helpless child in the care of such a man.

Del tried to be defiant, to catch Mr. Camden's penetrating gaze and make him look at her, but the longer she was in his presence, the more certain she was at how much vileness was hidden underneath his unassuming exterior. There was a quiet malevolence to him, his anger and short-leashed temper were almost palpable, and it made him seem so much larger and physically threatening than he appeared at first glance.

He studied Del, radiating frustration, and when he reached out to touch her face his grip was hard. Wordlessly, he tilted her head back, angling it beneath the light, and frowned at what he saw. From the pain throbbing in her temple and the stickiness of her hair, Del knew she was bruised and bloodied, and it obviously made Mr. Camden displeased. He checked her wrists, pulling at the ropes to see the wounds beneath, showing no reaction when Del gasped in pain.

"Bloody hell, Murphy," Mr. Camden muttered, and Murphy shrank back against the wall. "What do you propose I do now?"

Behind him, Murphy shrugged helplessly.

Mr. Camden hadn't spoken to Del directly or even met her eye since entering the room. It made her feel invisible.

She wanted to say something, to beg for her release or plead with him not to injure her further, but she held her tongue. Her silence stemmed partly from stunned fear, but also from a foolhardy defiance. As terrified as she was, as desperate as she was to escape her confines, she had never whimpered or begged a man for anything, and she would be damned if she would start now.

"I cannot let her go, not after what you have done to her," Mr. Camden said. "I cannot risk her telling anyone what has happened. She must be kept quiet, no matter the cost." He sounded casual, conversational, as if he were just thinking aloud, and that nonchalance chilled Del to the bone. He spoke of her fate, alluded to the possible violence it beheld, as though he were merely deciding on whether to dine on fish or fowl.

"I will say nothing," Del said, her words barely a croak from her dry and constricted throat.

"You have put me in a most untenable position, Murphy," Mr. Camden continued, showing not the slightest hint of having heard Del. "In your interminable stupidity and ham-handed incompetence, you have threatened this woman, struck her, and now dragged her to *my office*, my place of business, where you have bound her to a chair." Mr. Camden turned from Del and began to stalk toward Murphy, his motions deceivingly slow and unthreatening. Del knew better, and from the look on Murphy's face, he did too. Mr. Camden meant to do someone harm in retribution for this inconvenience, and Murphy was his target.

"She's jus' a whore," Murphy said in his defense. "Who'll listen to anythin' she says?"

Mr. Camden's back was now to Del, but she saw his shoulders stiffen and his hands clench at his sides, and she knew Murphy's words had only further enraged him. She knew what the elder Camden was thinking, that he hated being reminded of who and what his son had pledged to marry. Del silently pleaded with Murphy to shut up before his words damned her any further.

"I know what she is," Mr. Camden bit out. "But she has connections to some powerful men. And my son, if she ever told him—whore or no, she must be silenced."

"Mr. Camden, sir, I can take care of it." Murphy said, and if he was trying to come across as confident and reassuring, he succeeded only in sounding like a nervous, whiny child.

"And how, exactly, do you propose to 'take care of it'? I do not care for this—distastefulness. You are forcing me to get my hands dirty in a way I haven't in years." Mr. Camden's composure waivered ever so slightly, and Del could hear some of his rage come through in his words. She wondered what it would look like if he let himself explode. "You have put me in an impossible situation. She cannot stay here. She cannot be let go. What does that leave us?"

Del's heart slammed into her chest, and if she hadn't been restrained in a chair, physically prevented from moving, she knew she would have collapsed. There was only one option left open by Mr. Camden, an option he seemed disinclined to voice himself, but one she had no doubt he would see done. Not by his hands, of course, but by his bidding nonetheless.

Against the wall, Murphy visibly gulped. "I'll deal with it. Make sure no one sees nothing. Make sure the problem disappears."

Tears sprang from her eyes, and Del panted, trying not to become completely hysterical. The men were careful not to look at her and had ceased to even refer to her as a person. She was now a "problem" that needed disposing of, like spoiled cargo to be unceremoniously dumped in the Thames, never to be thought of again. Neither of the men said the word, and she knew they would steadfastly refuse to call her murder for what it was, but all their euphemisms wouldn't change the fact that she would wind up just as dead.

Her mind raced. She refused to believe this was her end, that there was nothing she could do. She would think of something. She had to. There had to be some overlooked means of escape or some perfect combination of words that would convince Mr. Camden to release her. Her muscles were tense, though, locked in place from abject fear and the physical pain of being tied to the chair. She couldn't move, couldn't make words come out of her paralyzed throat, could scarcely take in enough breath to prevent herself from fainting. She was running out of time and she couldn't *do* anything.

Mr. Camden stared at Murphy for several minutes, until the man squirmed and looked away. "We will leave her here until dark. When everyone is gone and you can move about unnoticed, you will remove her from the premises and make sure no one sees or hears of her again."

Murphy nodded, but when he looked about to say something, Mr. Camden cut him off with a raised hand and then gestured him out the door. Demonstrably bumbling but not completely lacking sense, Murphy left the room as quickly as he could without breaking into an obviously cowardly run.

The elder Camden then walked over to the table, the one Del had hoped contained her salvation, and picked something up before coming to her. Del's vision went dark around the edges and she grew dangerously lightheaded from the terror. He meant to do it now; he would kill her and have Murphy dump her body later.

"Please," she managed to say, the word barely a whisper, and she could say no more.

But Mr. Camden's hands didn't contain any implements of death or torture. Instead, he shoved a dirty rag into her mouth and secured it with a rope tied around her head, ensuring she would be unable to call for help. He knelt down to tie her ankles to her chair, cutting off the slightest chance of escape Murphy's previous oversight had left her. He stood up, having neither looked her in the eye nor spoken to her directly the entire time he was in her presence, and then left.

Alone in the dim and dusty room, Del cried.

The warm, salty tears ran in rivulets down her cheeks, and her sobs, muffled by the rag stuffed in her mouth, caused her to jerk against the ropes, further tearing into her flesh. She had no means of freeing herself, and Camden, not knowing where she was or what dangers she faced, would not be coming to save her.

She wept for the cruel sadness of it all, the unjustness of meeting her demise right after she had finally figured out the course her life was meant to take.

She wept for Camden, that she would be torn from him before she ever had a chance to really tell him what he meant to her. She loved him more than anything, and she could only hope that, even after her death, he would know it.

Memories of Camden flitted through her mind, and her tears flowed harder when she realized how much time she had wasted being stubborn. If only she had let her guard down in the beginning, right after meeting him, when she had seen him for the amazing man he was but had not let herself believe it. They could have had all those months instead of just the last few weeks when she had finally come to her senses. She had been so scared then, of feeling and loving and giving. It was all so wretchedly, comically clear to her now how wrong-headed she had been.

Her breathing became hitched, irregular. Her sobbing was leaving her gasping for air but the rag in her mouth was preventing her from getting it. Her vision went cloudy and her hands and feet went numb and she knew she was going to lose consciousness.

The last thing she thought of before the world went dark was Camden's face as he asked her to marry him, and the last thing she felt before losing all sensation was the stab of pain through her heart as she realized she would never be able to.

Chapter Ten

Camden walked along the corridor leading to his office. He was restless, distracted. Working today seemed an impossible task. He wasn't sure how he would muster up the motivation or interest in cargo manifests and pricing lists when all he could think of was Del. Of how beautiful she had looked this morning, tousled and thoroughly satisfied. Of how impatient he was to be with her again this evening, when he could take her in his arms, feel her soft body melt into his —

Gah. It was no good to think of her now, not when he was stuck at the shipping company and couldn't go to her. He was only torturing himself by conjuring up her image, by remembering the feel of her against him, under him, the way she moved and the way she sounded when he —

Dammit, he was doing it again. His head was filling with thoughts of her and his body was responding physically. He quickly thought of the stack of paperwork waiting for him on his desk. Nothing made the blood cool faster than the thought of slogging through piles of bills of lading and quarterly receipts.

In his reverie, he didn't notice the other man in the hallway until he had brushed past him.

Camden frowned. It was Murphy, one of his father's stevedores, and he had looked extremely unhappy.

Camden wondered if there was trouble. The stevedores usually kept to the docks and were almost never seen in the offices. If his father needed to communicate with one of them, he sent Camden or another employee to them rather than summoning them to building. The elder Mr. Camden didn't like having the austerity of his office sullied by the presence of the common laborer, as if their dirt and sweat and—*commonness* would cause his carefully created façade of wealthy respectability to come crumbling down around him and he would be exposed for the what he was: a desperate social climber of humble origins far closer to the stevedores than the blue-blooded aristocrats he aspired to become one of.

Camden stopped and turned around, intending to ask Murphy what his business was, but the man had already disappeared around a corner. Camden heard the creak of a door shutting behind him and he turned back in the direction he had been walking. His father was coming out of one of the records rooms, locking it with one of the myriad of keys he kept on him at all times.

"Ah, Rhys," his father said, looking startled to see him. He dropped the key in his pocket before walking quickly toward his son. Placing a hand on his shoulder, he steered his son back down the hall in the direction Murphy had gone. Camden allowed himself to be led. "I've been looking for you. Wanted to talk to you about a possible new account."

"Is that why Murphy was here?"

"What?"

If Camden hadn't known his father so well, if he hadn't become accustomed to reading the slightest expression changes and shifts in voice or stance or language, he may have missed the almost imperceptible reaction to his question. But he did catch it, how his father's eyes had widened just a touch, how he had given a small twitch, like he was going to abruptly stop walking but then caught himself and carried on. It had become a survival tactic for Camden, to notice the tiniest of details in his father's behavior as a way to gauge his mood and determine the level of danger he faced.

"Oh, Murphy. Yes," his father continued. "I was questioning him on whether he thought an addition of an account this large would necessitate hiring more stevedores."

"It must be quite the sizable account," Camden said.

"Indeed."

Camden tried to surreptitiously study his father as they walked side-by-side down the corridor. He wondered why the issue of a new account would cause his father to seem so guarded, so distracted, and he tried to find clues in the man's demeanor. Glancing at his father, however, showed him no insights. His father appeared to be his usual self: impatient, confident, with an ever-present aura of slight aggression and casual meanness. Camden could sense no more hesitation or surprise, and he thought perhaps he had imagined it all. It was Camden, not his father, who was feeling irritated and cagey, and he must have projected his own restlessness onto the older man.

He let out a frustrated breath. He hated having to be away from Del. His longing for her, his impatience for their nuptials, and his uncertainty regarding his father's approval of them was driving him mad and he knew it would only get worse as the day wore on, lonely and tedious and seemingly never-ending. It was distracting him, making him see trouble at the office and strangeness in his father when there wasn't any.

They reached his father's office, a large, Spartan room, impeccably organized. It was dimly lit even though there were six large windows extending from nearly ceiling to floor. The elder Camden kept them shuttered at all times, as if convinced the sunshine would destroy his machine-like productivity and drive for success. Heaven forbid he let any light into his life, either metaphorically or literally. He instead relied on a single gas lamp resting on his desk.

There were books, ledgers, and papers everywhere, but unlike in Camden's office, where they occurred in haphazard heaps strewn across every horizontal surface, here they were coded, stacked and lined up in neatly organized piles on his huge desk. There were no pictures, no portraits of relatives or painted tableaux of calming pastoral domesticity. Nothing that would personalize the office, enliven it, or hint at a life outside it. The entire room was like a physical representation of the man who kept it: willfully restrained, relentless organized, devoid of ostentation or anything resembling softness or comfort.

Mr. Camden went to his desk and sorted through the piles of documents. There were no chairs to sit in, a deliberate choice to keep visitors from becoming comfortable or staying too long, and so Camden stood awkwardly by the door, waiting for his father to give him further instruction.

"Here," Mr. Camden said, placing several thick folders of papers in his hands. "Take these to your office and read through them. They contain all the information of the possible new contract. Prepare a prospectus outlining the relevant issues, the costs, labor and equipment needs as well as all the possible profits and net gains of taking on the client. I'll have it by this afternoon." He sat down at his desk, waving his son out of his office without another glance in his direction.

Camden shifted his weight self-consciously. He knew the prudent thing to do in the face of a dismissal from his father was to run and do his bidding, but he wanted to bring up the issue of his marriage. It wasn't the perfect time, of course, but there was rarely a good time to discuss anything with his father, and he was impatient to have things resolved. His father never looked up from his desk, however, and Camden was once again feeling a strange agitation from him, and so he decided to go to his office and get to work. Things were sure to go more smoothly for him if he engaged his father in discussion *after* handing him a meticulously prepared report that would, he hoped, show a significantly favorable outcome for the company. The prospect of huge financial gain was the one thing that went the furthest to put his father into any kind of mood resembling amenability.

Once sitting at his own desk, Camden threw himself wholeheartedly into the project. He welcomed the chance to concentrate on something other than Del and how much he wanted to be with her right now, since there was nothing he could do about it at the moment. The facts and numbers contained in the files were dry, straightforward, and numerous to the point of being almost overwhelming. Because there was almost nothing he hated more than sitting indoors sorting through this type of information, he had to force himself to give it his full attention. It meant there was no opportunity to torture himself with imagining, in exquisite detail, exactly what he would do to Del if he were with her. Stuck at the office, those fantasies would do nothing but frustrate him both physically and mentally, and it was better to concentrate on other things until he could go to her tonight and act out every last decadent thought he had ever had about her.

The distraction worked, for when he looked up from the papers in front of him to give his tired eyes a rest, a glance at his pocket watch told him several hours had passed. He was stiff from sitting so long in an uncomfortable chair and he took a moment to stretch his arms and legs. He needed to take a break from work to move his limbs and perhaps take a meal, and so he decided to ride to Del's townhouse and invite her to eat with him.

Outside, astride Sebby, Camden was immensely glad of his notion to leave the offices for a bit. The afternoon was beautiful, with clear blue skies with a gentle breeze containing just a hint of autumn crispness. The trees were showing their golden, crimson, and brown colors, and already a few leaves had fallen to the ground, crunching beneath Sebby's hooves. It was a perfect day for a picnic in the park, and Camden deeply regretted he had only limited time for a visit with Del before returning to work to finish his prospectus.

As he approached Del's townhouse, his entire body warmed in anticipation of seeing her. Perhaps he would forgo the suggestion of a meal and instead invite Del to partake in sating a far more primal hunger. His appetite was voracious when it came to her, like she was his ambrosia, the only thing capable of sustaining him. It was difficult to remember he needed anything else when he was around her. Air, food, and water seemed like inconsequential nuisances when his senses were filled with her heady scent, her luscious curves, her beautiful voice.

He bounded up the stairs to her townhouse, all eager anticipation, but stopped short when he saw her front door was just slightly ajar. He frowned. Del was always thoughtful and organized and it was entirely unlike her to be so careless. He pushed the door open while calling her name, his heart beating a slightly faster tempo. The residence was quiet. There was no response to his repeated calls to her. He walked through the foyer, trying to ignore the feeling of worry creeping up on him. No need to be worried just yet, he assured himself, Del had probably gone out, perhaps to see Jane, and had simply not noticed the door had not shut completely.

And then he saw it.

A heavy candlestick lay on the floor. When he picked it up, he saw it was smeared with something that looked very much like blood. The hair at the nape of his neck rose, his palms began to sweat, and his heart pounded. Violence had been done here, he thought, violence against Del, and she could now still be in danger.

He tore through the house, shouting her name, trying to keep his fury and worry from completely overtaking him. The edges of his vision went red, like it did whenever his anger rose, and he wasn't sure he could keep it at all contained this time. He had no idea what had actually happened here and he tried to stop his mind from conjuring up a myriad of horrific scenarios. Surely there was a perfectly reasonable explanation for the open door, the seemingly bloody candlestick, and Del's absence, one that involved a minor lapse of memory and a moment of clumsiness or something similar. He tried to make himself believe that, but he couldn't shake the feeling of dreadful surety that whatever explained what he saw here would be decidedly *un*reasonable and not at all minor.

Upstairs, Camden saw the unmade bed, the tousled covers still suggesting the outline of where they had lain together. He saw a pair of gloves and a reticule on the bureau. She wouldn't have left the house without such things, but he didn't know if she had others she had taken instead. His agitation and panic increased. He hated this uncertainty, hated feeling like Del was bleeding and hurt and beyond his reach, but then not knowing if that were even the case.

Camden had searched the whole house and found nothing, no sign of Del and no clues to point him in any definite direction. He decided he needed to return to the foyer and check closely and methodically for something—anything—that would shed light on what had occurred and give him an idea on where to look for Del.

He noticed the table that stood against the staircase wall. The various items resting upon it were in disarray, as though someone had knocked them over or perhaps bumped—or been shoved—into the table. There were a few drops of blood on the floor near the table and a few more near the door. He tried to focus on the fact that the presence of minimal amounts of blood suggested only minor injuries, but the very implication of any injuries at all was driving his anger and worry to dangerous levels.

His eye caught on something small and dark lying on the floor in the shadowed corner near the front door.

It was glove. A man's glove.

It was made of thick leather, darkened by age and dirt and scuffed from heavy use. It was no finely stitched riding glove of a gentleman but rather the utilitarian glove of a workman, and it had no earthly reason to be in Del's house.

The sight of that glove destroyed Camden's hope that nothing untoward had happened to Del. A man had been here and it had not been merely a pleasant social call. The visit had resulted in disturbed furniture, a candlestick apparently used as a bludgeon, blood, and his missing fiancée.

Camden's fear and rage and righteous vengeance began to take over him—and he let it. He welcomed the rushing blood and throbbing temples and tightened muscles of his shaking fury. A man had come here and hurt Del. Perhaps it had been a random burglary attempt and Del had merely been unlucky to have been targeted. Or maybe it was premeditated revenge from someone she knew. He thought of Ashe, how angry he had been when Del ended their arrangement, how he had leveled threats and laid hands upon her. Had he or one of the other men had become enraged upon hearing of her engagement and come to forcefully change her mind? The exact motivation didn't actually matter, for Camden would hunt down and punish the perpetrator regardless of who it was or what he wanted.

He needed to control himself, to clear his mind of the dizzying anger just long enough to formulate a plan for finding Del. He would go back to the shipping office and enlist several of his father's men—as well as Wittingham, Farber, and Hollsworth—to form a searching party, and they would go to every damn house and building in London until they located her. They would start with Ashe and go from there.

And when he found Del, may God show mercy to the poor soul responsible, because Camden sure as hell wasn't going to.

• • •

She was running.

It was early morning, but the heavy cloud cover meant it was cold and damp and gray. The fog hugging the ground was so thick it seemed like a solid, impenetrable wall that would stop any forward progress. She slipped through it though, her legs pumping, until the tattered hem of her sleeping gown wrapped itself around her knees and threatened to trip her. Her bare feet slapped against the cold, jagged cobblestones of a neglected and deteriorating street.

She ran faster.

Her breathing was heavy, her lungs burned, and her fatigued muscles were in danger of giving out completely, but she could not stop or even slow her pace. She was being chased by dark and foreboding things. She couldn't see them but she knew they were behind her, swallowed in the fog, just out of sight.

She was terrified—of what was coming after her, of what was lying in wait ahead, of her own weakness and exhaustion and diminishing ability to ever find safety.

There were voices behind her. Women were shouting at her, criticizing and scolding and threatening. Men were jeering and cajoling, making specious promises and impossible demands. It was all an almost intelligible cacophony of hostile pursuers and she needed to be free of them.

She ran blindly, not knowing what obstacles or hazards lay in her path, not knowing her destination or whether salvation even existed. She would not stop, though. She would continue to run, alone and cold and afraid, until she either found a place she felt safe or collapsed from the effort of trying.

The cobblestones changed beneath her feet. She was running on grass now. When the fog suddenly lifted and the sun peeked through the clouds, she saw she was in a meadow. The voices behind her were muted, far away, and she slowed to a walk, grateful for the chance to rest. There was a man in the distance standing under a tree. She realized she knew him somehow. She needed to reach him, and then she would be safe and happy and protected. Each step that brought her closer to him also brought a feeling of absolute calmness, and she felt she couldn't get to him fast enough.

She began to run again, but this time is was *to* happiness and joy instead of away from fear and misery.

She was almost there. She was so close to him she could smell his slightly musky scent, see locks of his hair tousle in the breeze, see the deep, rich brown of his eyes. He reached out to her. She lifted her hand to him, but just before their fingers touched the distance between them suddenly and jarringly increased. She began to panic again, that familiar cold knot of fear coiling in her stomach. She called out to him, wanting to know why he was abandoning her just when she had finally found him. Before the words were formed, however, she realized he wasn't the one moving away. *She* was sliding backwards, as if pulled by an invisible rope, and soon the fog behind her would swallow her completely.

The discordant voices of her tormentors grew louder. She was again almost within their grasp.

It was too much.

She was too tired, too frightened, too alone to fight anymore, and she contemplated ceasing to struggle and just accepting her fate. It would be so easy to let the fog take her, to give into her fears and doubts and let those who wished her harm do what they may. It was seductive, the urge to give up, to end the pain and terror and bone-deep weariness of constantly running, of always fighting.

Tendrils of fog curled around her ankles. Her vision became blurry and her limbs grew numb. She knew if she did nothing, she would soon disappear completely. Her thinking slowed, her body felt weighted down, and she prepared herself for whatever awaited her in the foggy nothingness.

But then she caught a glimpse of him, off in the distance, the man who was her everything. He had been there a long time—she knew it in that way of dreams and nightmares—waiting for her to come to him. He was her happiness, her safety, her respite from any cruelty or loneliness or injustice.

She would fight her way to him. She would struggle against the fog and the fear and the doubt until she left it all behind forever when she finally reached his arms.

She needed him and he needed her, and she wouldn't give up until they were together.

And so Del opened her eyes.

It took a moment for senses to clear, to determine if she was awake or still dreaming, to remember what had happened. Her stiff, cramped muscles, her difficulty in breathing around the rag in her mouth, the pain in her ankles and wrists, it all brought the reality of her situation back to her in a hurry.

She had been slipping away. The blow to her head was making it difficult to stay awake, and the rag in her mouth made it hard to get enough air. It made for a dangerous situation, and if she hadn't fought her way back to consciousness when she did, she would have never awoken again.

She knew she needed to fight to stay conscious until she found a way out of this room. Until she could escape her bonds, or draw the attention of someone who could let her go, or convince Murphy to do it when he returned. One of those options would work. It had to. She was so clear now in what she wanted and who she needed. She loved Camden unreservedly and whole-heartedly, and that knowledge brought her serenity and strength rather than uncertainty and self-doubt.

She only hoped the opportunity for salvation appeared soon, because she didn't know how much longer she could hang on.

Chapter Eleven

When Camden finally reached the shipping offices, both he and his horse were in a full lather. He had been working through his plan and that had helped to keep the anger and panic and bay, but he hadn't been able to completely tamp it down. He would gather as many of his father's men as he could, split them into several groups, and dispatch them to different parts of the city. While they were already on the search, he would go round to fetch Wittingham and his other friends and get them to join in the effort. He needed as many men as possible to be effective in finding Del. It was at least a small comfort that he knew where to start.

He headed straight to his father's office. Camden needed his permission to pull the men from their labor and send them out on searching parties. He took deep breaths as he marched down the corridor, trying hard to regain some of his composure. He needed to be calmer and more collected when he faced his father, not appear the red-faced, wide-eyed, enraged maniac he was at the moment. Otherwise, his father would waste precious time reprimanding him for his lack of self-control when he really needed to be focused on finding Del.

He was relieved to find his father's office door open. It meant he could be reasonably justified in striding into the office without knocking and waiting for an invitation to enter.

"Father."

Mr. Camden looked up from his desk and frowned at his son and Camden knew from that expression that he had been largely unsuccessful in composing himself. He was still breathing hard, every muscle was clenched, his hands were fisted at his sides, and he could only imagine what expression he was wearing on his face.

He was wild with worry, tense with anger, and he looked it. He was barely keeping himself in check. His father did not approve.

"You have finished with my prospectus?" Mr. Camden looked pointedly at his son's empty hands and Camden understood the implied admonishment. He had no business being out of his office if he hadn't yet completed his task. Already, his father was annoyed with him.

"It is almost finished. I just—there is a situation, and I need—"

"What are you blathering on about? What situation could you have possible run into while working in your office?" Mr. Camden's voice hinted his words were only part question, part reprimand, and all impatient disdain.

Camden tried to quickly come up with the best way to describe what had happened and what he needed, as if there were specific words that would trigger a compassionate, helpful response from his father. Realizing that was futile, he settled on brevity. "Del has been kidnapped, and I need as many of your men as possible to help me find her."

For at least the second time that day, Camden noticed a strange reaction in his father—a small jerk of his head accompanied by a dark glower. Camden could tell the man hadn't meant to let his displeasure show so obviously by how quickly he schooled his features into an impassive mask. It confused Camden that his father would allow anyone to see such an involuntary reaction, no matter how briefly. Not that his father had any problem letting his anger or disapproval be known, just that it didn't usually come in the form of small jumps and startles instead of a measured and purposeful response.

Camden brushed it aside. There was no time to worry about what his father was thinking. "I need your permission to gather the men from the docks and form searching parties."

"Absolutely out of the question." Mr. Camden sounded incredulous that his son would even suggest such a thing. "I am not pulling the men from their duties to send them off traipsing pointlessly around the city. Not when it will accomplish nothing but a wasted day of labor."

Camden was about to press his case when he stopped himself.

He closed his mouth and took a step back, his body going cold. Something in what his father had said, in the *way* he had said it, sent a jolt of horrified suspicion down Camden's spine.

"How do you know the search would be pointless?" Camden spoke the words very carefully, his voice low and biting. "How do you know it will accomplish nothing?"

Camden saw a flash of unexpected uncertainty in his father's eyes before the man's familiar mask of dangerous irritation slammed back in place.

"I do not *know* if the search will prove fruitless, I am simply not willing to sacrifice a day's work to find out," his father said carefully but firmly.

Mr. Camden sounded again like his usual malevolent, authoritative self. He spoke as if there was nothing left to discuss. But it was too late. It had been in his father's eyes when Camden mentioned Del. He had heard it in his father's voice when he declared the search pointless. Camden saw it in his father's stiffness and the way his eyes darted from Camden to his desk.

His father knew.

He knew Camden would find nothing if he searched for Del throughout the city. He knew it because he knew where Del was, because he was the one responsible for her disappearance.

Camden's breath caught and his mind reeled. His heart slammed against his chest. His skin dampened with cold perspiration. It seemed so obvious now. His father hated Del and what she was. He hated that his son wanted to marry her, so he had made sure it could never happen.

"What have you done with her?" Camden barely recognized his own voice. It was deep and gravelly, with no hint of equivocation or deference.

"I do not like your tone," Mr. Camden warned. "I do not like what you are accusing me of."

Camden took a step toward his father's desk. His blood pumped through his veins, his muscles tightened. Everything about him was taut, ready to spring. "What have you done with her?" he repeated even more forcefully. "Where is Del?"

"Enough of this ridiculousness!" Mr. Camden stood from his chair and planted his hands on his desk, leaning forward. It was the posture he always adopted when he was trying to intimidate, but Camden barely noticed. "I will not stand for the insinuations and accusations. Stop engaging in fantasies. Go back to your office and finish my prospectus and do not let me see you until it is done!"

There was a part of Camden—the part of him that was still the small, scared boy he had once been—that wanted to obey his father's commands. He felt it pull at him, a little voice that spoke to him of fear and consequence and duty, and he almost retreated.

But he fought it.

He dug deep into that part of him that was now a man, that loved Del and needed her and would do anything to find her and keep her safe. The part that would stand up to years of lecturing and threats and escalating violence and would defy the father who still had the power to intimidate him.

"I will not leave." Camden spoke each word slowly and carefully. "Not until you tell me what you've done with Del."

His father's eyes widened and his face went red. He tensed to the point of vibrating. Camden saw the emotion boil in him, the anger at being questioned, the rage at being defied.

"What does it matter what's happened to her? She's just a whore!" his father spat. "She's probably run off with any one of a dozen random men. And good riddance! To think you wanted to marry her, to sully our name and degrade our station by attaching yourself to such a creature."

Camden looked wordlessly at his father, a feeling of unreality taking over him. It was as if he were looking at something that could not exist, that defied all laws of nature and went against everything known to humanity. His father was yelling at him, a note of shrillness creeping into his voice, and Camden couldn't be moved to care. All he could think of was how he needed to find Del. How his father had to tell him where she was so he could go to her and make sure she hadn't been taken from him forever. It was the only thing that mattered. All his father's disappointment and judgment, all his anger and commands and threats, it meant nothing to him now.

"You will tell me where she is." Camden closed the distance between him and his father in a few long strides. He planted his hands on his father's desk, mimicking his father's stance, and God help him, the man actually took a step back. "You will tell me now."

His father began to sputter incoherently, too surprised or enraged to form actual words. Camden was about to repeat the commands, to lean in further and raise his voice and *even lay hands upon his father* if necessary to make him talk, when it struck him. He remembered earlier in the day when he had encountered his father in the corridor. He had been coming out of the records room and when he saw Camden, the briefest look of guilty surprise had crossed his face, like he was a boy caught pilfering sweets.

Del was in that room.

His father or one of his men had gone to her townhouse, struggled with her, and brought her here where his father had locked her in that room. He didn't know exactly what his father had hoped to accomplish, but Camden knew she was there with the surety and infallibility of his love and devotion to her.

Without another word to his father, Camden turned on his heel and left the room. He stalked down the corridor, fighting the urge to break into a panicked run. He was barely aware of his father behind him, chasing him down the passageway, shouting at him to stop and cursing him for his perfidy. If he hadn't been so utterly preoccupied with desperate worry for Del, Camden would have been completely gob smacked by the unprecedented absurdity of the scene.

He finally reached the records room, his father right behind him, still yelling. He called out Del's name and tried to open the door, but it was, unsurprisingly, locked. Camden whirled to face his father and was about to demand the key from him when he was met with a hard slap across the face. It stunned him for a moment, the sudden and unexpected violence, and Camden staggered back a step.

"Stop this right now!" his father yelled.

Camden blinked at him. The man was completely out of control now, wild-eyed and shaking in fury. Camden had never seen him like this. Even at his angriest, even when meting out his most violent punishment, his father had always been controlled and methodical. Now he was like a mad man gone unhinged.

"Get back to your office!" His father was almost screaming now. He brought up his hand, preparing to strike again.

Camden didn't stop to think. He was pure reaction now. He wasn't Camden, the dutiful son; he was a man desperate to reach the woman he loved. That wasn't his father, a man to be obeyed; he was nothing more than a threat to that woman's safety and an obstacle to her rescue.

Camden grabbed his father by the lapel of his coat and propelled him backwards. He slammed him into the wall, lifting him off his feet. He let go, and his father fell to the floor. Camden cocked his fist back, ready to strike, prepared to beat his father into a bloody mass, when some semblance of sentience returned and he stopped himself.

He looked down at the man, trembling in fear on the floor, and Camden wondered why he had ever been afraid of him. Had his father always been so small? Had he always seemed so shrunken and shrill and ridiculous? Why had he ever let this man rule over his life? Why had he ever wanted his approval so desperately, fought so hard to avoid his disappointment? George Camden was nothing, just an empty shell of a bitter and lonely man.

Camden dropped to his haunches and his father shrank back against the wall at Camden's nearness. Ignoring him, Camden reached into his father's waistcoat and withdrew his ring of keys. Without another glance at the man who had once loomed so large in his life, Camden rose and went back to the door. There were perhaps a dozen keys on the ring, and Camden, in his desperation to reach Del, didn't have the patience to try each one. Throwing the keys to the floor, he stepped back and then launched himself at the door, dropping his shoulder and putting his full weight and rage behind it. The door heaved and he heard the wood crack and split. One more hit and the door gave way in a flurry of chips and splinters, and Camden burst through the gaping hole.

Del was sitting in a chair in the middle of the room, her wrists and ankles bound to it. Her head was down and her long, unbound hair hung in her face, obscuring it. For one numb, agonizing moment, Camden wasn't sure if she was still alive. But then she moved and Camden could breathe again.

He rushed to her, murmuring her name. He knelt beside her and put a hand under her chin. He gently brought her head up, brushing her hair back so he could see her face. He gasped when he saw it, how she was gagged with a filthy rag, how her eyes were half-open as she struggled to stay conscious, how her hair was sticky and matted from a bloody cut just above her eye, how that eye was puffy and swollen from a hard blow viciously dealt. His rage came back full force. The blood pounded in his ears and his vision went dark and he was consumed with the urge to go back out to the corridor and beat his father until he was unrecognizable.

With a great and purposeful effort, he calmed himself. Going after George served no purpose. His father was a useless man and beating him would do nothing to help Del. And that was what mattered. Freeing Del, getting her out of here, and tending to her wounds was the only thing Camden cared about right now.

He untied the rope holding the rag in her mouth. "Del. Del, honey, can you hear me?"

"Camden," she said, the words barely escaping from her dry, cracked lips.

"I'm here."

Camden worked to untie the knots binding her to the chair. He was beyond frustrated at how his shaking hands made freeing her difficult. He wanted to rip the ropes from her wrists and ankles but he could see they were already bruised and raw, and he would kill himself before causing her any more pain. Finally, the ropes were undone and Del was free. He lifted her from the chair and gathered her to him, taking just a moment to revel in the feel of her against him.

"My God, Del, I was so worried I had lost you," he murmured.

"You haven't," Del said, choking back a sob. "You're here." She spoke as though in wonderment, as though trying to convince herself he was real.

Camden squeezed her against him, battling his own emotions. He needed to be out of here, away from this place and his father and the temptation to exact vengeance upon him. He needed to get Del somewhere quiet and safe where he could tend to her and perhaps be convinced she was really all right.

He rose, still cradling Del in his arms, and left the room. In the corridor, he stepped over the still supine George and walked out of the shipping offices, never once sparing a backward glance for the broken man heaped on the floor.

•••

Del held her breath. The touch of the wet rag to her bloodied wrist hurt, but she tried not to wince because it greatly upset Camden whenever he saw signs of her pain. Even with her effort, however, she wasn't able to completely hide how tender her injuries were.

Camden stilled his hands as soon as she moved. "I'm so sorry for hurting you," he said, his voice full of worry and concern.

He was frowning, brows knitted, with such a stricken look on his face that Del smiled weakly in an attempt to comfort him.

"It isn't so bad," she said.

"Let me fetch the doctor. I don't know what I'm doing and I'm afraid I'm only making this worse."

"No," Del said, struggling to sit up in her bed, getting tangled in the bed covers and her nightgown.

"Shhh," Camden said. He took her gently by the arms and eased her back against her pillows. "Don't exert yourself."

"You're almost done cleaning the wounds and bandaging them," Del reasoned. "There is no need for the doctor. And certainly no need for the questions and suspicions this is sure to cause."

"Damn whatever suspicions he has. I will deal with him. What's important is making sure you're well."

"I *am* well, truly." Del put a hand on Camden's arm, and she felt some of the tension and frustration leave him at her touch. "A little bruised, yes," she added when Camden had been about to speak. "But it's nothing rest and time won't heal."

Camden looked at her wordlessly, and Del knew he was deciding whether to let her have her way. In the end, he simply resumed washing her wrist and binding it with a clean, dry bandage. He would let her win, for now at least.

Once she was completely cleaned and bandaged, he went to fetch water and then sat back down on the bed beside her to help her drink. He put the glass down and brought his hand to her cheek, studying her.

"Bloody hell, I was scared," he whispered. His voice was so quiet Del wondered if he had even meant to speak out loud. "When I came here and saw the blood and the man's glove—when I realized you were gone—I was so terrified I wouldn't be able to find you, or that if I finally did, it would be too late."

Del placed her hand on his. "It wasn't too late," she said, trying to calm him. "I wasn't going to leave you. I was fighting to find a way back to you, and then you came."

"But if I hadn't come, if I hadn't figured out what happened—" Camden shuddered.

"You did come, though. We fought our way to each other."

Camden looked at her, his eyes round from emotion. "I'm so sorry." His voice was full of quiet agony. "My father, what he's done—"

Del reached out to touch his face. "No. It's not your fault. What he did, he did on his own. You couldn't have known."

"But I should have. I should have known what he was planning. I know him, how he thinks, how he reacts. I should have guessed what he intended." Camden pulled back and turned away, looking overcome with guilt, afraid to meet her eye. "He's always thought himself entitled to demand certain behavior from people. I've seen him seek his revenge whenever someone fails to do what he demands. I *knew* he didn't want me marrying you. I've experienced his retribution often enough, I should have known what his disapproval meant. I should have protected you." Camden turned back to her and gathered her in his arms. "Forgive me for not protecting you." He hugged her tightly, as though loosening his grip or letting her go would be to risk her disappearing.

"You've done nothing to forgive." Del took his face in her hands, made him meet her eye. "You did nothing wrong."

"But I have!" Camden released her and rose from the bed. He paced the floor of her bedroom like a caged animal with too much pent up aggression. "I've spent my life trying to appease that man. I've let him run my actions and rule my emotions. He's been vicious and cruel my entire life, and still I've nearly worked myself into my grave trying to appease him." Camden paced faster, clenching and unclenching his fists in frustration. "I've sacrificed so much—my time, my friends, my dignity, my autonomy—in the vain hope that it would gain me—*something*—some small measure of approval, of—of the *slightest* sliver of love from him. But it's gotten me nothing, not even a reprieve from his unrelenting censure. And now—now I almost lost you." Camden sat back on the bed and took Del's hands in his. "And now I must be done with him."

Del forgot sometimes how young Camden was. He was mature, yes, and had the self-possession of a much older man, but he was still only twenty-one. He was still struggling with what it meant to be a man. He was still pulling away from his childhood and the power his parents had over him and learning what it meant to be a person, fully formed and independent of them. Del had been forced to leave childhood early and stand on her own, and she knew it was never easy. It was a process full of pain and self-doubt, and the difficult relationship Camden had with his father only complicated things.

"Oh, Camden, to sever ties with your father completely—"

"I must do it. I *want* to do it. For my sanity and for your safety. My father and I are nothing but poison to each other, and I want to be free of it. I have spent far too many years in the fruitless endeavor of trying to be his son, and it's ended badly for all of us. I refuse to allow you to remain in danger and my father is nothing but danger for us both. I will not risk you or your happiness. I am through wasting my time on him."

Del nodded. She knew what it meant to be locked in a battle with persons who represented nothing but pain and degradation for you, and she knew how cathartic it was to finally free yourself from them. It was a monumental thing to walk away from a family member, but she would support Camden if he needed to do it.

Camden kissed her gently, sweetly. "I'm just glad I found you and we're together once more. I'll never let another thing get in our way." He kissed her again.

"I'm so sorry there ever was anything keeping us apart," Del said.

The guilt returned to Camden's face. "I know, I—"

"No, not you. I meant me, how I kept myself at a distance, how I let my fears come between us."

Camden looked confused. "What do you mean?"

"I spent so much time trying to protect myself, to guard my precious independence and freedom, I didn't even notice that I had built a cage for myself, had cut myself off from everything that mattered. Love, friendship—you. I held myself back from you, even after I knew what you meant to me and how much I loved you." Tears filled her eyes and spilled down her cheeks. "I'm sorry, Camden, I'm sorry for how, in my foolishness, I squandered so much of our time together. What terrifies me is how I almost didn't have the chance to atone for it."

"So we've both been foolish."

"Yes, and we almost let that foolishness keep us apart. For so long, we've been beholden to our fears, imprisoned by the expectations of ourselves and others."

Camden picked her up, so very, very gently, and placed her on his lap. He smoothed her hair from her face and dried the tears from her cheeks, placing soft kisses there instead.

"No more," he said. "It seems we are finally free, together."

Epilogue

Del hummed to herself as she added the long column of numbers. A heady warmth suffused her body, the after-effect of a morning spent with her husband that had yet to dissipate. Almost a year after their wedding, she still thrilled at calling him her husband, still reacted with heated readiness when she saw his face or heard his voice. Every time with him was like the first time, and she hoped it always would be. Their passion never abated, their giddiness with each other never subsided, and she didn't think it ever would.

Del tried not to get too distracted with thoughts of her husband, but they always intruded no matter what she was doing, no matter how pressing her work. Something always reminded her of one of their late-night conversations whispered to each other in bed, or of the feel of his naked body against her skin, or of his laughter when she said something to amuse him. The smallest thing would bring up the memories of any of the thousand looks or words or touches they shared and she would want to drop everything and go to him. She wanted it now, but she needed to stay focused and finish the accounts and so she deliberately banished from her mind the images of them together that morning.

Camden always hated the bookkeeping and preferred to be outdoors, but she found the numbers comforting. They were logical and predictable. Two plus two always equaled four. There were no surprises in the math, nothing unexpected. It soothed her to sit in her cozy office and track expenses and income, to file receipts and organize their records, and she was good at it.

She had finally succeeded in turning her full attention to the accounts when she heard the creak of wheels and the jangle of tack outside. She looked out her window to see a carriage coming up the long drive to their home, and the sight made her smile. It would be either Wittingham or Jane, as they were both expected to arrive sometime today for an extended visit. Putting aside for a moment her excitement to see old friends, she finished her addition, checked her numbers one last time, and then closed the ledger. Work was done for now.

She went outside to find Camden, knowing he would want to greet the arriving guests. She found him exactly where she expected: in the small side paddock working a chestnut colt on a lunge line. She stood for a moment, just watching him. His blond hair was tousled, his shirt and breeches dusty, and he looked utterly gorgeous. He was loose-limbed and relaxed, with an expression of carefree joy on his face. Outside on their land, working with their horses, it was the happiest he was when not with her, and Del could stand and watch him all day.

He turned to look at her, breaking into a wide smile at the sight of her, and Del's heart melted just a little. He was so beautiful, so kind and amazing, and she still couldn't believe her luck that he was hers.

"Come to help me, my dear?"

Del shook her head, smiling at his address, and gestured to the front of the house where Wittingham was alighting from his carriage.

"Right. Seems you are granted a reprieve for the day," he said to the colt. He removed the lunge line to let the horse scamper free about the paddock, and then he leapt over the fence in an easy, fluid motion to join his wife. Taking her hand in his, he led the way to greet their friend.

"Ho, Wittingham!" Camden called. The men clasped hands and slapped each other's backs in the age-old gesture of male affability and affection.

Wittingham bowed to Del and smiled at her in greeting. "Mrs. Camden," he said, taking her proffered hand for a genial kiss. "You are looking well."

"I see you've made the long journey to the uncivilized north relatively unscathed," Camden said.

Wittingham frowned at him. "If you call a wretchedly sore ass, a pounding headache from riding over the pitted monstrosities you call roads, and clothes covered in more wrinkles and dirt than an old naked man in mud pit 'unscathed,' then yes, I've got here just fine." Wittingham made a great show of straightening his impeccable cravat and dusting off his sleeves.

Camden laughed and gave his friend another playful punch, which made Del laugh, and then even Wittingham couldn't stop himself from grinning.

"I'm surprised you could bring yourself to make the trip," Camden teased.

"Yes, well, I've need for a new horse, and I hear you breed the finest specimens in England. I expect an exceedingly good deal, of course."

"You will have to speak to my wife about deals and discounts. I just breed the horses, she runs the business aspects of it all. I'll warn you not to get your hopes up, however. She is a shrewd negotiator that could talk a miser into paying *her* to take his goods off his hands. You will likely pay full price and more, and never be happier doing it." Camden leaned down to kiss Del's cheek, his admiration showing clearly on his face.

"Oh, Camden, stop," Del said, laughing. "I have never dealt unfairly with anyone or cheated them their due, and you know it."

"Cheated them? Never. You have a way of making people willingly and happily give over everything to you. As I have." Camden looked at her meaningfully, and Del blushed under his gaze. He wrapped an arm around her, drawing her close, and she leaned into him. They were losing themselves in each other, as they always did, and would have forgotten Wittingham completely if he hadn't cleared his throat pointedly.

"Ah, yes. Let's get you inside and settled before we talk business," Camden said, gesturing to a footman to unload Wittingham's things from the carriage. "William will show you to your quarters, and when you're ready, I'll show you around the grounds."

Wittingham followed the servant into the house, and Del turned to go inside as well, but Camden caught her hand and stopped her.

"I meant it, what I said." Camden looked down at her earnestly, encircling her with his strong arms. "I've given everything of myself to you, happily and willingly." He kissed her, the gesture tender yet strong.

Long ago, when Del was another person in another life, someone had told her she was like an orchid under glass. That she was closed off and anyone trying to reach her faced only jagged edges and injury. That she was delicate and fragile and would curl and wither at the slightest pressure and so she held herself back from others, walled off lest they caused her harm. Trying to be with her only resulted in the destruction of them both.

Here, now, standing on their land in her husband's embrace, she realized she had become an orchid *made* of glass. She was open, transparent, everything about her freely shown. She was enduring and unable to be crumpled or bent; she would hold up to the bruising pressure of others. For hers was a heavy, toughened glass, and while still smooth and beautiful, it made her deceptively strong. If hit with just the right blow, yes, her edges could crack, but she would never completely shatter and her essential core would hold.

"And I am yours, completely," she said, kissing him back.

She marveled that there had ever been a time when such a declaration would have filled her with fear and a sense of weakness. Now it gave her confidence. She had her own strength, and with the addition of her husband's loving hands around her, she could withstand anything she faced. He wouldn't let her fall, wouldn't let her break, he would temper any of her remaining vulnerabilities.

With him, she was invincible.

About the Author

Emma Barron lives in upstate New York with her family and two dogs. When not writing, she's usually chasing her daughter, starting house projects she makes her husband finish, or killing all the plants in her garden. Learn more about her at *www.emmabarronbooks.com*, find her on Facebook, or follow her on Twitter *@barron_emma*.

A Sneak Peek from Crimson Romance
(From *One Night's Desire* by Rue Allyn)

Wyoming Territory, Late May 1870

From the back of her mare, Kiera Boudicca Alden peered through the cloud covered night at the horses lazing in the corral of the Flying V ranch. The frenetic activity from the party going on inside and around the main house didn't seem to bother the horses, but it bothered Kiera, almost as much as the angry voices coming from the direction of the horse barn. "Ain't no way, I'm letting you run off with her," one voice snarled.

She couldn't hear the reply, but a moment later she did hear gunshots.

She sidled her horse closer to her Shoshone companion. "Muh'Weda, we've got to get out of here," she whispered.

"If they're arguing about some girl, they're too busy to notice us, and we need to get those horses back."

Kiera made one more attempt to convince her spirit brother that his plan would lead to disaster.

"I'm all for you gaining enough *puha* to convince Aishimite'Bui's father that you'll make her a worthy husband, but you could have found a less dangerous way to do it than stealing your ponies back from the most powerful rancher in the territory."

"This way is best. The greater the risk, the greater the *puha*. Besides we're only taking a few horses. With all the noise those whites are making, they'll never notice. Come on." He nudged his horse forward.

Kiera had little choice but to follow where her friend led. She was here because of that friendship, but she very much feared someone would see the horses being taken from the corral and assume she and Muh'Weda were rustlers. Rustlers were shot on sight or, if captured, hanged.

Their unshod Indian ponies made little sound as they slipped through the shadows toward the barn.

"I don't like this," she muttered so only Muh'Weda could hear. "Do you smell smoke?"

"No. If there was smoke the horses would panic. You find the three mares and lead them out," whispered Muh'Weda as he unlatched the corral gate. "I'll get a rope over the stallion and be right behind you. Remember, if we get separated, I'll meet you at the weeping rock near the Big Horn."

"But…"

Before she could object, he was through the gate and swallowed by the now stirring equine mass.

Under the waning moon the night was dark. How was she supposed to find three specific mares out of more than fifty in the wooden enclosure? Her photographer's eye supplied accurate memories, but she took photographs in clear daylight, not darkness. Muh'Weda seemed to think she'd have no problem. She rubbed the scar on her left temple to ease the ache of tension and ignored the itchy feeling at her nape. Then she recalled the image of the horses she'd photographed nearly a year ago and started searching.

With every moment in the corral, she got more and more tense. By the time she found the three mares, her skin prickled, her head pounded, and an icy sweat formed on her brow. Unease spread through the herd like wildfire. She sniffed the air. Now certain she smelled smoke, she managed to get the mares on leads and headed toward the gate then glanced about to locate Muh'Weda. She found him, but he was too far away to hear any warning she might call. Her hand was lifting the gate latch when a horse trumpeted in anger.

She turned her head to see the stallion rear, hooves flailing. A break in the cloud cover sent a weak moonbeam to light the taut line strung from the irate stud's neck. Kiera traced the line back to where Muh'Weda fought to control the stallion and haul it closer. Thank heaven the gelding her friend rode was well trained and sought to help its rider by casting its weight backward.

The nearer Muh'Weda drew the stallion, the louder its snorts and bellows became. Stirring increased among the rest of the horses. Outside the corral a growing commotion added to the noise. Shouts and screams echoed over the milling horses and the still resistant stud.

"They're stealing the horses!"

"Get Big Si, the sheriff, and Marshal Quinn!"

Acting on instinct, Kiera shoved the gate open as wide as she could. Then with the mares' leads in one hand, she pulled her pistol and galloped through the opening, firing into the air as she went.

The entire herd followed, raising enough dust and confusion to hide both her and Muh'Weda—if he could get the stallion under control and escape the corral.

•••

"Excuse me, miss." At the sound of gunshots and shouting, U.S. Marshal Evrett Quinn pushed from the house onto the veranda, passing Miss Elise Van Demer. Whatever the young woman wanted to tell him would have to wait, no matter how upset she seemed.

He cleared the porch railing to land beside his horse at the hitching post amid the chaos of running, shouting men and women.

"The barn's on fire."

"How'd that happen?"

"Who cares? Let's put it out first."

"I saw two Indians stealing horses from the corral."

"Form a posse."

"We need to put out the fire."

"Get Big Si. Where's Sheriff Boswell, and the Marshal?"

"Last I saw, the sheriff was headed to the horse barn, just before the dancing started."

Ev did a quick scan and found Big Si Van Demer astride the platform set up for dancing, but found no sign of Boswell. The rancher was built like a stonewall, tall and heavy set. He had a booming voice that cut through the rising panic, bringing quick order if not calm. Ev mounted his horse and headed toward the platform.

"You there," the rancher pointed at a hired hand. "Get these people organized into a bucket brigade. Then get four of the hands to haul out and set up those fancy hoses I had shipped in from Chicago."

The order was followed immediately with a good thirty people lining up to pass water from the creek to the fire.

Ev knew he wouldn't be fighting the fire. If he wanted to get the horse thieves, he needed to start now and couldn't wait for the fire to be extinguished or to find the sheriff. Besides, Sheriff Boswell knew these ranchers and townspeople. He, better than Ev, could keep folks from forming a lynching posse. Ev was pretty sure no rustlers were gonna set a fire as a distraction and risk a stampede, which could prevent them from getting the horses. He didn't think for a minute that the same person or persons set the fire and stole the horses.

Big Si's next order went to his foreman. "Take any man not fighting the fire and round up the stray horses. I'm not losing that Army contract because of a couple thieving Indians."

"Si, I'm going after those rustlers," Ev interrupted.

"Boyd!" Si shouted for his newest hand.

Ev had met the man just that night and hadn't liked what he saw. Known only as Boyd, the hand had a lanky whipcord build and eyes constantly on the move. That, the low-slung six-shooter strapped to his thigh, and the careful way he carried himself implied that Boyd was more gunslinger than cowpoke. When they'd shaken hands, Boyd's were soft, like a city boy's.

"Here, sir." The man stepped out of the bucket line and approached Si.

"Get your mount and go with Marshal Quinn. I want my horses back."

"And the rustlers?" asked Boyd.

"They're murderers. Do what you were hired to do."

Ev frowned. He knew Big Si's temper and had no doubt that the rancher wanted the rustlers shot, but Ev didn't operate that way. With the sheriff—who hadn't struck Ev as being on friendly terms with Si—occupied, Ev was the only lawman available. Van Demer's insistence that the gunslinger join the pursuit made Ev wonder if there was more to this than simple horse stealing. Determined to catch the thieves alive, he attempted to avoid the offered help. "I can't wait for him, and you need every hand you can get to fight that blaze. I'll leave a clear trail for Sheriff Boswell to follow once the fire's under control."

Flames from the burning barn lit the cold grin that struck Boyd's face. "I'll catch up."

Ev shrugged. He'd have to find another way to keep Big Si's man from killing the rustlers. He pushed the gunslinger from his immediate thoughts and urged his horse into motion. Firelight reflected off the dust cloud from the escaping horse thieves. Ev headed in that direction, knowing that was where he would pick up the rustlers' trail.

• • •

For the past three days, Kiera and Muh'Weda had managed to stay ahead of their two pursuers, stretching their lead to almost a half a day. However, getting the lead had cost them. They were lost.

Under the noonday sun, Kiera lifted her hat and swiped at the sweat trickling down her forehead. Oh, she and Muh'Weda both knew which direction would lead them to his village—west, but they were headed east. The idea had been to hide their tracks in the first stream they came to then double back, losing the pursuers in the process. However, every stream they found was little more than a mud track that would leave clearer prints for the pursuers to follow. So the pair had pushed on until now, when they paused to let the horses drink from a puddle that hadn't yet dried up.

The badlands stood before them. Kiera knew better than to enter the twisting, endless chasms. They'd lose all sense of direction within an hour, and once in, the chance of getting out of the rocky maze alive was miniscule—better to risk facing the two men who'd followed all the way from the Flying V.

"We're going to have to deal with them," Muh'Weda's statement drew her from her thoughts.

"Lord knows we can't seem to outrun them, and places to hide are few and far between."

"My father told me that Chief Washakie once said 'if you must fight, it is best to choose the time and battleground'."

"We can't fight them. I may be able to fire a pistol, but we both know that my hands shake so much from fear that I couldn't hit the sky if I aimed at it."

Her friend grinned. "I never could figure out why you're afraid of guns when you're not afraid to live alone in Smoke Valley."

"Solitude doesn't scare me, but guns…I saw a man murdered once and haven't been able to fire a weapon accurately since. I've got other ways to defend my home, just like you taught me other ways to hunt."

"True. Still I'd like to hear the story of the murder someday, so I can really understand."

"The story and my fears won't matter, if those men catch us. They think we're rustlers, and they'll hang us at the first tree they come to."

"Then we'll just have to make certain they don't catch us."

"How?"

Muh'Weda shrugged. "Beats me."

"Wonderful." Kiera shook her head. Out of loyalty she'd allowed herself to be dragged into a situation where she could very well lose her life. She'd never see her sisters—one older, one younger—again. All the dreams she had of reuniting with them and bringing them west to live in her valley would die with her.

Though she mourned the loss of her dreams, she didn't regret helping her friend. She'd been on the run for most of the past three years; the last eighteen months in Wyoming had been harsh. She'd been slowly freezing to death in the Wind River mountains when Muh'Weda found her. Until then, she'd not dared to hope for reunion with Edith and Mae. It was Muh'Weda's help and his family's kindness that allowed her to finally feel safe and settled enough to hope. She hadn't escaped her grandfather's brutal plans then survived three years of tribulation and disaster just to surrender and die. She'd get herself and Muh'Weda out of this, if she had to bushwhack the pursuers. "That's it. We'll set up an ambush."

Muh'Weda stared at her, his jaw flapping. "Why didn't I think of that?"

"You did." She couldn't let her friend feel inadequate. He'd never get the *puha* he needed, and that had been the main purpose of this adventure. Getting back some of the village horses was an added benefit. The real gain was in proving to the village and the elders not only that getting the horses back could be done, but that Muh'Weda could do it.

"I did?"

"Sort of, you said we should choose the time and place for the fight. What's an ambush if not that?"

"Did you have anything specific in mind?"

"Yes. I'll tell you all about it while we look for the right kind of canyon to use as our battle ground then find a spot to leave our horses and the other ponies."

• • •

The sun hung low over the horizon when Muh'Weda scrambled into place beside Kiera behind a large rock fall that created a choke point in the box canyon where they'd set their ambush.

To someone unfamiliar with her Shoshone friend, his thin lips and flat features made it seem as if he were dead serious. However, Kiera saw the twitch at the corners of his mouth and the sparkle in his eyes. He was as excited by the coming confrontation as she was.

"They're following the trail we left and should be here soon."

"Did you get the stallion and the mares secured in that other canyon?"

"Yep. They're too far away to be easily heard but close enough for us to get them without any trouble if our plan works. The men following us will think we lost the mounts and are stranded."

"It better work. I don't like the alternatives."

"Me neither."

She handed him her hat then tied a bandana over her bright pinned up hair. "I'd better get moving, so we can spring our surprise."

Her friend smiled, but the sparkle faded. "Be careful, Kiera."

"You too."

Swift and silent she hurried into position behind a boulder just inside the mouth of the canyon. She signaled Muh'Weda when she was in place and watched him arrange her hat to make it look as if she were still with him. Then she hunkered down to wait. She would stay hidden until the men settled into a spot for their attack on what she hoped they believed were two rustlers.

She and Muh'Weda had chosen this canyon because the chasm's mouth was well out of gun range, which made that opening the most logical place for the pursuers to leave their horses. Separating the men from their mounts was key to the success of the plan.

From behind the rock, she watched the two men leave their horses tied to a low branch growing out of the canyon wall then make their way, one on each side of the chasm, toward a tumble of rocks about twenty feet from where her hat showed Muh'Weda's position to be. She was now between the men and their only exit.

One of the men wore a badge and was on her side of the canyon. He signaled the other man to hold off firing. However, the second man either didn't see the signal or ignored it and aimed a careful shot that blew Kiera's hat off the rock.

Darn. I liked that hat.

Muh'Weda returned fire fast enough to make it seem as if two people were taking careful shots at their pursuers.

Quick and quiet Kiera eased from boulder to boulder toward the horses. At the last rock she checked to see that the pursuers' attention was focused on Muh'Weda. Choosing her moment, she broke cover and ran for the steeds left near the canyon mouth. Her job was to take possession of the horses. Then, using the mounts as cover, she would help Muh'Weda, by threatening the two men from behind. They didn't need to know that she couldn't hit a target and only carried a gun to complete her disguise as a man.

Once she and Muh'Weda had the men in what appeared to be crossfire and they realized that aiming bullets in her direction would kill their horses, the men would surrender and the gunfight would be over with everyone alive.

She'd put her foot in the stirrup and hoisted herself halfway into the bay gelding's saddle when something grabbed her free leg.

There was no sight or sound of the stolen horses, but both rustlers hid behind the boulder where the bullets came from, so Ev wasn't certain what caused him to turn and look toward the canyon entrance. However, the itchy sensation that signaled unseen danger attacked his neck.

"No!" He holstered his gun and sprinted for the horses. One of the desperados was trying to steal their mounts. "Keep him pinned down," Ev yelled to Boyd.

"What?"

Ev prayed the gunman would figure it out because explanations would have to wait. Before the rustler swung into the saddle, Ev managed to get a grip on the desperado's foot and pull hard.

The horse sidled away, and the man tumbled backward. Swinging his arms and twisting as he fell, he landed smack on top of Ev. They toppled to the ground with the rustler astride Ev's chest. The man was a lightweight and would never have knocked Evrett down without the momentum from the horse's movement.

He lifted his arms to fend off a punch, but the punch never came. Instead, his opponent's arms flailed, hands slapping, fingers gouging and scratching. One blow landed on his ear and set his head ringing.

Damn, this guy fights like a girl. Ev attempted to get a grip on the wildly swinging arms, but they seemed to be everywhere at once. Unable to stop the assault, Ev shot his arms straight out, under the area where the suspect flailed, and shoved at the assailant's chest.

The move sent the thief flying to land butt first in the dirt about two feet away. The startled expression on his face was quickly replaced by a feral snarl.

Ev shook his head to clear it. Had he felt breasts beneath the rustler's shirt?

That moment of wonder cost him as the man—or was it woman?—leapt for him.

This time Ev was ready. He gripped his attacker at shoulder and thigh, lifted, and tossed the suspect away.

A satisfying 'oof' sounded as the man, or woman, hit the ground back first and lay still as stone.

Ev stood and waited.

His opponent was so much smaller, that standing, he—or she—wouldn't have a chance of beating Ev in a fist fight.

The suspect coughed and heaved in a breath, then another.

Ev studied the face and bone structure, the slight build. The distinctive white blonde hair straggled out from a covering bandana framing lake green eyes and a mouth too generous for any man but just right for a woman. "Geezus in a dress. You're a female."

The smile that mouth formed dazzled him, but the eyes remained hard. "You noticed that, did you?"

Her husky voice struck him like the punch he'd expected earlier. He felt embarrassment creep up his neck. "Uh, kinda hard not to when I, uh…" he looked at his hands before holding one out to help her up.

"Well, then let me return the favor."

He quirked an eyebrow in question.

She grasped his extended hand and used it to pull herself to her knees where she hauled back and plowed a fist into his crotch.

Ev crumpled like a wad of paper, writhed on the ground, and moaned in agony. "Why?" he managed to croak.

"I noticed you're a male."

"You all right?" An Indian dressed Shoshone style, asked the question. He held a rifle on Boyd.

Still in pain, Ev looked from the woman to the Indian and back.

"I'll be fine." She rubbed one hand at a scar on her left temple then folded her arms across her chest. Her shoulders hunched as if to relieve some sort of pain. She tossed her head in Boyd's direction. "How'd you get him?"

The Shoshone grinned. "He ran out of bullets before I did. When he tried to sneak off, I got the drop on him."

"Well I'll be damned." The gunman stared at the woman. "What about you, Marshal Quinn? You okay?"

"I'll live, but I won't be walking for a time. What are you gonna do with us?" If he was a dead man, Ev wanted to know.

"We're not going to kill you, if that's what you're worried about," remarked the woman.

"Matter of fact, that did concern me some."

"Help your friend move over to that rock." The Shoshone gestured Boyd to a nearby boulder. "Then sit down with your backs to it."

Boyd helped Ev hobble to the rock.

"Here's your gear." The woman had removed the saddles and other equipment from both Ev's and Boyd's horses. Keeping the weapons and ammunition, she dropped the rest beside Ev. "We passed a way station about a day and a half walk from here. We'll leave your horses there. You'll find your weapons and ammunition under the deadfall half a mile east of this canyon."

The Shoshone helped the woman to mount one of the unsaddled horses before scrambling atop the other.

Ev watched the two ride off.

"Well if that don't beat all," remarked Boyd. I sure as hell wouldn't leave an enemy behind me, 'specially not with weapons he could use against me."

"They're young. Maybe they don't have enough experience to know better."

"That's just plain stupid. Don't take experience to do the smart thing."

Ev gave that some thought. He never would have left an enemy with access to weapons. 'Course, in his line of work he didn't leave enemies behind. His job was to bring them in and lock them up. The only reason he could think of for leaving the weapons was so that two men on foot wouldn't be completely defenseless. The woman and the Shoshone weren't stupid, which left kindness as the most likely motive for leaving the weapons behind. Somehow the thought rankled. The woman clearly didn't like him. Shoot, she'd punched him in the nuts and knew damn well he wanted to send her to jail. Why in God's name would she do anything kindly toward him?

Ev shrugged. "Who knows. Maybe they aren't murderers."

"They were smart enough to leave our gear to slow us down," muttered Boyd, looking with disgust at his heavy saddle. "And they set that fire at the Flying V to cover up the murder of Sheriff Boswell. Between the bucket brigade and those newfangled hoses, Si managed to save most of his barn, and Boswell's body was still recognizable."

"That gear will help us stay alive. Thieves starting a fire at the same time they're stealing horses doesn't make sense. The horses would spook. If they murdered the sheriff, why not murder us? Leaving us alive makes even less sense, if they've already killed." The thoughts made Ev more curious than ever about what was going on. More and more this incident looked like something other than simple horse thieving.

"You've got a point. 'Sides, what kind of horse thief leaves two good mounts where the owners can find them?" wondered Boyd.

Ev wanted an answer to that question too. He sighed, slung his saddle and gear over one shoulder then commenced walking. He was gonna be mighty footsore by the time he reached that way station.

"So why, d'you suppose, is she traveling with a Shoshone?"

"She?"

"Yeah, she, the blonde woman."

"How'd you figure her for a woman?" He looked at Boyd.

The gunman smiled. "Well, I watched you tussle with her, and she sure doesn't fight like a man. And, no man I know wears a face like hers."

Ev couldn't quite figure why he should be bothered by the fact that Boyd noticed the blonde was a woman. He wanted time to sort out all the thoughts swirling around in his head and wished the gunslinger would stop talking.

Boyd kept on talking. "Then too, the Shoshone helped her onto your horse. If he did that to another healthy man it would be an insult."

"You know, for a gunslinger, you sure talk a lot. Ask a lot of questions 'bout a woman Big Si wants you to kill, too." Ev tried to stare the man into silence.

Brows lifted slightly, Boyd returned Ev's gaze. "Maybe I don't plan on killing her. Si doesn't know one of the rustlers is female. Even if he does cotton to killing womenfolk. I don't. As for conversation, where's the harm? Didn't know not talking was a requirement for being able to hit what I shoot at." He uttered the rebuke in a level, almost cheerful tone. "Not all folks in a profession behave the same. For instance, I know at least one lawman who can laugh."

Ev couldn't restrain a smile. "That'd be me, right?"

Boyd rolled his eyes. "Ah, yeah, right."

Ev nodded and pondered the benefits and risks of trusting Boyd. "C'mon, let's catch those two and get some answers."

He lengthened his strides, and for the first time, Boyd fell silent. Unbidden, the image of the blonde woman came to Ev's mind, and a queer sort of tension curled in his chest. He wasn't certain what the feeling meant other than that he wanted to get his hands on her. He forced the image from his mind and kept walking. No woman was going to do what she'd done to him and get away with it.

•••

When Kiera and Muh'Weda, their string of ponies trailing behind, finally rode into the Shoshone village near the shore of Lake Yellow Stone the entire population came to welcome them. As Muh'Weda dismounted, three girls broke from the crowd, rushing to hug him and hang on his shoulders. "Yes, I am happy to see you too."

Listening to him murmur endearments to his sisters, Kiera smiled and slid from her saddle. Family would occupy her friend for some time.

A hand on her shoulder had her turning to see the well-worn face of Spirit Talker, the band's elder medicine man.

"Welcome home, Dabai'Waipi—Sun Woman. Our prayers have been answered. You and Muh'Weda have returned safely, and we have much to celebrate. Muh'Weda has proven what the elders could not decide—that it is possible to get our horses back from the white rancher who stole them."

"We only took four horses." Leading her mount and the other four horses, she walked toward the village corral of scrub and branches.

"True." Beside her Spirit Talker nodded sagely. "But you brought our stallion, which we badly need, and three fine mares— one of them is in foal."

"She's not showing yet." Kiera knew better than to ask how Spirit Talker knew about the mare's condition. If the medicine man wanted her to know, he'd tell her. Spiritual leaders held positions of great respect in the Shoshone community. The stronger the spiritual power, the greater the respect. The principle was similar to a Shoshone man's *puha*. The term had no equivalent in English but had much to do with a man's personal power and the community's respect for him.

"She will soon enough, and the colts she bears will be mighty war horses."

"We may need those war horses sooner rather than later. Along with the four ponies, I'm afraid we may have brought a great deal of trouble for the village." She curried her mount and put the gray into the corral of wild brush. Closing the barrier, she turned to study Spirit Talker.

"You are wise for such a young woman. Trouble is coming, but not in the way you believe. The white man's army will stop the rancher from attacking us, and eventually we will get all of our horses back. Now, I have taken too much of your attention for myself. Others wish to greet you."

Together they returned to the main part of the village.

Spirit Talker caught her arm before allowing her friends to surround her. "When you are done here, my daughter and I will assist you and Muh'Weda at the sweat lodge."

"Ah, so we will celebrate tonight. Thank you for thinking of our needs."

"Of course," the old man smiled. "But before that we will eat, and you and Muh'Weda will tell of your adventures.

Kiera turned from Spirit Talker to greet her friends and was soon engulfed in hugs and backslapping. She was a bit embarrassed, for she hadn't gone with Muh'Weda for glory. She'd only wanted to help a friend and had hoped to talk him out of an action that—despite Spirit Talker's assurances—could very well bring more trouble than the horses were worth. Nonetheless, she accepted the praise of the villagers, for she loved and admired them. To reject their thanks would be churlish and rude. They believed her deserving, and that was all that mattered.

Soon enough she emerged from the crowd and waited on the edge for Muh'Weda to finish his greetings. He loved his sisters as much as Kiera loved her own, and she would not grudge him a minute of the time he spent with them. What did it matter, if she missed her family a little more on this occasion or if an empty place in her heart held nameless longing.

Unbidden the face of the marshal came to mind. Honey brown eyes that might melt a woman's heart, if kindness ever shone in them. Thick, feathery red hair just a shade off copper that looked soft as a dove's wing. A three day shadow of the same hue softened the sharp planes of his face. Long, lean, broad and strong. Strong most of all, in both body and mind. For even when she'd struck him where it hurt most, long moments passed before he fell. The promise of retribution in his hard gaze had grabbed her and shook her, refusing to let go even when she was weak and limp inside. Because their encounter had been short and not an occasion for smiles, he should have been frightening. Nonetheless, her mind conjured a grin on that beard-shadowed visage.

Quinn, that's what the other man had called him. He was a U.S. Marshal, with both personal and professional reasons to hunt her down like a rabbit. She'd do well to remember that. Thankfully, a full month would pass until she had to leave the mountains to get supplies. She hoped the marshal would give up searching for her long before then, but she wouldn't take any chances. She was prepared to fight if need be, although she'd much rather not. Distraction had always worked best for her, so she'd do what she could to change her appearance and make herself unrecognizable. She'd done it before; she could do it again. Her photographer's eye for image and the tricks learned in San Francisco would help. When she went for supplies, she'd test the result on Muh'Weda. If she could fool him, she could fool anyone.

In the mood for more Crimson Romance?
Check out *Lady Broke*
by Rachel Donnelly
at *CrimsonRomance.com*.